Conflict at Hanging Rock

Pauline Wilson

Boughyards Press

First published by Boughyards Press in 2022

PART ONE

Chapter One

1849 Beguildy, Wales

H arriet dashed over towards the pen where her husband was tending the sheep. She waved a letter in the air.

"Come quickly, Albert," she cried. "It is a letter from Robert."

Albert looked stunned.

"A letter, from Robert. Does that mean they have set him free? We have had no letters before."

"I don't know Albert, I haven't read it yet."

"What are you waiting for?"

Harriet and Albert went inside and sat down at the table in their poorly furnished home. Harriet opened the letter and began to read.

Dear Father and Mother,

You will not believe the good fortune that has befallen me. After two years spent in hellish conditions in Pentonville prison, I have arrived here in Port Phillip with a ticket of leave. Can you believe it? I am basically a free man. And after only 2 years in prison.

They loaded us onto a ship, the Maitland, all 300 of us. It was a terrible journey. But that is a story for another time. We expected to be sent to Van Diemen's Land and continue our sentences in the penal colony there. But we landed instead at Port Phillip and they gave us all our papers. The reason, they said, was that they needed workers here to help the pastoralists look after their sheep. I still need to report to authorities, and I am not allowed to leave the colony, but I can work for myself and earn a good living.

I worked first in Melbourne and then came out to the interior of Port Phillip District and got work with a wonderful couple, Benjamin and Esther, on their sheep farm.

The best news is that I now have land of my own! I have built a hut and have a flock of sheep and a horse. And I am growing potatoes. It is hard work in a harsh place, but I am doing very well.

But to get to the reason for my letter. I think you should all join me here. There is enough land for us all to have a share. I have heard that there are passages available to South Australia. That is a fair distance from where I am in Port Phillip, but it would not be hard to continue on from South Australia to join me. I have done well since I have been here, so I am sending money to help you obtain a passage.

Please, please consider it! And please send a reply care of the Macedon District Post Office.

I remain your obedient son,

Robert.

Albert and Harriet stared at each other in shock. It seemed unbelievable to think that Robert was not only safe and well, but that now he owned land. It was news they could only have dreamed of. Could they join him? It all seemed quite impossible.

As they let the news sink in, Harriet's mind went back to the day that she would never forget, when her precious youngest son Robert had been convicted of larceny and sentenced to transportation.

1844 Beguildy, Wales

Harriet cringed as they led Robert to the dock, chains at his ankles and wrists, his face ashen and his round hazel eyes wide with fear. Her son was not a tall lad, standing only 5 foot 6 inches, a diminutive figure behind the spikes of the dock, just 19 years of age. He was charged with larceny at the Quarter Sessions in Radnorshire.

The public area was crowded, as usual, with sensation-seeking townspeople pushing and shoving to get a better view and jeering as they brought each new prisoner to the dock. Today there were many farmers amongst the crowd, wanting to see justice brought down on those who had stolen their property.

It is so unfair, thought Harriet. *If the landlords and the government had treated us fairly, my sons would not have needed to steal.* Robert had been trying to help their starving family and instead here he was, charged with an offence that was likely to get him locked away for years. Michael had already been convicted and was, as far as Harriet knew, on his way to Van Diemen's land to serve a 10-year sentence. She held her breath as the Chairman read the charges.

"You are hereby charged with stealing a quantity of wool. Do you understand the charge?"

"Yes, My Lord," answered Robert.

"How do you plead?"

"Guilty, My Lord." It was no use denying the charge. Harriet hoped that by Robert pleading guilty the court might show him some leniency.

The Chairman asked the prosecutor, a local farmer, to give his account of the offence. The farmer stood and read his statement.

"I had gathered a flock of my sheep together, ready for shearing. When I returned early the next morning, one of the sheep had been shorn. I then gained intelligence that the wool would be found at a nearby warehouse. I am convinced that the fleece found in that warehouse was indeed from my sheep. The warehouse owner told me one Robert Blayney, the accused, had sold it to him."

The jury filed out of the courtroom to deliberate. They were not gone long.

"How say you gentlemen of the jury?" said the Chairman.

"Guilty, My Lord," replied the jury spokesman. The verdict had been short and sharp, and the sentence was handed down just as quickly. The Chairman shifted in his seat and delivered the sentence.

"Robert Blayney, you have been found guilty of larceny and you are hereby sentenced to 7 years transportation."

Harriet's knees buckled as the verdict was read. She felt the tears form in the corners of her eyes. It was likely that she would never see her son again. As Robert was led away, she caught his eye and attempted a small smile, hoping to give him some strength.

1850 Beguildy, Wales

Harriet sat by the open fire stirring the pot, the contents of which somehow had to stretch to feed the entire family. To the water she had added what little barley meal she could spare, a turnip and some salt. She sighed as she thought of Robert, far away in Port Phillip. The letter sat propped up on the shelf above the open fire. He wanted them all to pack up and leave everything they knew, to join him in a harsh new land. The family had talked of little else since the letter had arrived.

A farm on his own land. It was unheard of here in Radnorshire. The family lived in the small rural township of Beguildy, surrounded by mountains. The land they farmed was rich and in a good year would produce well. But it was not theirs. And never would be. They worked so hard. But they had to rely on the good graces of the landlord to allow them enough from what they grew to make a living. They also had to pay tithes to the church. Each time the rent was collected, Harriet wondered if they would be able to make the next payment. She knew there was a possibility that they could be turned off this tiny piece of land at any time and if that happened, they would all be separated and forced into the workhouses, where conditions were even worse than what they were experiencing now. She could not bear the thought of being separated from her husband, Albert, let alone her remaining children, even though they were all grown. Already her two youngest sons, Robert and Michael, had committed crimes which had seen them in court and sentenced to transportation. And she was sure that Charles could easily be next. He was the oldest and Harriet thought that he was a bit too sure of himself. It was really only luck that none of his escapades had so far landed him in front of a magistrate. She did not worry so much about

George as he had learnt a trade with which he was at least able to make ends meet.

Harriet and her husband Albert shared their tiny, thatched roof stone cottage with two of their children. They had partitioned off three rooms with woven branches daubed with mud so that they all had some small amount of privacy. She and Albert slept in one room, their daughter Rebecca in another, and Charles had a makeshift cot set up in the corner of the main room. The rest of the room was sparsely furnished with a table and chairs where they ate. Pots and other cooking implements surrounded the open fire. There was a more comfortable chair by the fire where Harriet spent any spare time she could as her bones became weary with age and the hardship she had endured. Now in her 61st year, she was thankful that Rebecca had never married, as she was a great help with the household chores. Above the chair was a small shelf which held Harriet's most prized possessions, her few tattered books and now Robert's letter. It was a poor home with not much to recommend it, but it would still be hard to leave.

Harriet knew they could not keep on the way they were. Was this their only chance? Should she and her husband pack up their remaining family and try to get a passage to this far-off land? Robert had said there were passages to the new colony of South Australia.

Whilst Harriet stirred the watery soup, Rebecca busied herself setting bowls and spoons on the table. Then she cut small chunks off the meagre loaf of bread, sighing as she did so. Harriet felt sorry for Rebecca. She was the oldest of Harriet's children and her only daughter. There was nothing here for her. Perhaps she could find some happiness if they left Beguildy.

Albert came into the cottage after ten hours working in the fields to get seed in the ground in good time. They had had poor season after poor season with no improvement in sight.

"Should we leave Albert?" whispered Harriet as she ladled the meagre soup into a bowl and added a piece of dry bread to her husband's plate to supplement his meal.

"This is our home, Harriet," replied Albert. He was a man of habit, and Harriet knew he would take some convincing.

"But Robert has land, his own land. Can you believe it? We could do well in the new country. Charles and George could come with us. There is land enough for all."

"But just to pack up and leave everything. I've heard tell it is a long and harsh journey," said Albert, still far from convinced that this was a good idea.

Soon Charles, a strong young man, not yet beaten down by the hard work and repression that was taking its toll on his father, arrived for his meal.

As Harriet dished up his meal, he joined in the conversation. Charles was a spirited young man who was keen to stand up for his family's rights. To add to all the other costs the family faced, there were now tolls on the roads as well. The Blayneys and their neighbours relied on the roads to take produce to market and to cart lime to improve their soil. Charles had joined the protests against the turnpikes. It was dangerous to be involved in these protests and Harriet worried for him.

"We will never beat the tyranny here," Charles declared. "I say we go!"

"What about George?" asked Harriet. "Do you think he will want to come with us? He is settled and has taken up with a young lady". George was a tailor and had moved to the larger centre of Edgbaston to further his career. From his frequent letters to his mother, she knew he was doing well, much better than they were all faring here on the farm. She wondered what he would think of leaving everything he knew to sail to a far-off land.

"I am sure George would want to come with us," said Charles. "I know he has steady work as a tailor, but he is still of very little means. If he had better prospects, I am sure he would ask Susannah to marry him."

It was frightening, but Harriet felt that to leave their home and join Robert was the only option. Over the ensuing weeks, she found out all she could about the passages that were available. She read the newspapers and spoke to neighbours who were also considering this course of action. Some had family members who had already taken the leap of faith. She knew there were agents appointed by the British government to assist people who wanted to emigrate, and she read the pamphlets they published. Their local pastor had helped her to find an agent who could assist them in getting a passage to South Australia. She told her family about all her discoveries as she found out more and more about the opportunities that were available.

Then she took a trip to Edgbaston to talk to George. George's first thoughts were of his love. "I don't know that I could leave Susannah," he said sadly, although deep down he craved adventure and the opportunities that might be on offer.

"Susannah could come too," said his mother gently. "You should marry that young woman. You have kept her guessing for too long already."

George blushed but said no more. His mother knew that he secretly longed to marry Susannah, but wondered what he could offer her. If they made this voyage, then there could be hope, but Harriet did not know whether the young woman would agree that leaving Wales and everything she knew would be such a good option.

Slowly, Harriet convinced her family that this was the right thing to do, the best option, perhaps their only option. It really boiled down to going or staying here to face a premature death from overwork and starvation. Albert eventually came around to her way of thinking. She wrote to Robert to tell him the news that they had secured a passage and with luck, they would disembark in Adelaide sometime in August or September. She promised to write again from Adelaide when they arrived.

George had raised the subject with Susannah and to his surprise and delight, she was very much in favour. He asked her to marry him, and she agreed without hesitation. The marriage took place at St Bartholomew's church in Edgbaston. A small gathering of family and friends toasted the newlywed couple. Their friends and neighbours also celebrated the approaching voyage that the family was to embark on. Many of them would have given anything to be in the Blayney's place.

1850 Liverpool, England

The momentous day had arrived. The family stood on the pier in Liverpool with their trunks packed with their few simple possessions. Harriet could not help but be fretful about what the journey would hold and how they would reunite with Robert when they arrived. They would still be hundreds of miles away from his farm.

The Blayney family walked up the gangplank to the deck of the sleek new ship, the Albatross. The sails flapped in the wind. The crew moved hastily around the decks, preparing the ship to sail.

The first part of the journey went smoothly as they sailed down the west coast of Africa. But as they approached the equator, they found themselves in the doldrums. There was not a breath of wind for nearly three weeks. When the passengers were on deck, they stared up at the limp sails, willing them to move. The family despaired that they would ever make it to their new home. And to make matters worse, Susannah fell ill and had to be tended to by the ship's surgeon.

"Did we make the right choice?" Harriet spoke quietly to her husband, Albert.

"Oh, lass, you must keep your chin up," he replied quietly. "This calm can't last forever. I spoke to the doctor, and he satisfied me that once we make landfall, Susannah will recover quickly." Still, Harriet could not help the sense of foreboding she felt. If this was not a good move for her family, she would never forgive herself for talking them all into it. She was tense with anxiety as they waited for the wind to blow.

Eventually, the wind picked up again and they were on their way. Harriet felt relieved, but she hoped the journey would not take too much longer. As the ship approached the Cape of Good Hope, the seas boiled, and they all became extremely ill from seasickness. They were glad to dock at Cape Town and have some respite for a few days whilst the ship took on supplies. Once the ship got under way again, they all felt much better as they benefitted from the fresh food and water taken on at the port.

The long days at sea dragged on and on. But then, just as they were beginning to think they would never reach the new colony, a flock of birds appeared on the horizon.

"Look Albert," cried Harriet. "Birds! Surely this is a sign that land must not be far off."

"Yes, lass, I believe you could be right," replied Albert. "We haven't seen any other birds since we left the Cape."

"Oh, thank goodness. I am not sure how much longer I can last on this cursed ship."

The appearance of the birds buoyed the passengers and a cheer went up. Hearing the commotion, Charles, George and Susannah joined Harriet and Albert on the deck.

"Well, I don't think it will be long now, mother," said Charles. "I am sure the birds are a good sign."

And sure enough, after 150 long and treacherous days at sea, they sighted the vast colony that would become their home. The ship sailed around the south coast and into Port Adelaide. The family surveyed the port from the ship, looking around in wonder and some trepidation. It was a busy port with many immigrants arriving, mostly British but also many Germans.

Harriet and her family stepped ashore amid the bustle. The heat was like a blast from a furnace. They soon became hot and uncomfortable in their heavy clothing. Now that they were off the ship, they no longer had the cooling effects of the sea breeze. They all stood in shocked silence as they surveyed their surroundings. The landscape was colourless and dry as far as they could see. Everything around them was unfamiliar, from the trees and plants to the heat and dust.

Their meagre belongings had been brought ashore and now they needed to find someone with a cart who would be willing to take them and their belongings to find some accommodation. As they stood looking around, helplessly wondering what to do, a pleasant-looking young man approached them.

"Need some help?" he called cheerfully.

"Yes, actually we need some transport," replied Albert.

"Well, it seems you are in luck. I have a horse and cart here for just that purpose."

They loaded their trunks onto the cart and Albert and Harriet joined the driver whilst the others walked alongside.

"Thank you for agreeing to transport our things. Can you suggest somewhere we could find accommodation?" asked Albert.

"My brother and his wife run a pub in town. I will take you there and you can see what they have to offer."

Albert and Harriet went into the pub with the driver, who introduced them to his brother.

"Welcome," said the publican. "Yes, we can certainly find a couple of rooms for you and your family. And you can store some of your trunks in the stable at the back if you need to. Where are you heading?"

"We are intending to travel to Port Phillip District. We have a son there and we hope to join him on the land."

"Well, there are ships sailing almost every day. It shouldn't be too difficult to get a passage."

"First, we must get a letter off to Robert to let him know that we have arrived," Harriet reminded Albert.

"That shouldn't be a problem," said the publican. "If you get the letter to me, I can make sure it goes by the first available mail."

Although they had some remaining from the money that Robert had sent them, they were eager not to spend what little they had. The next day, thinking of saving their money by getting to Port Phillip as soon as possible, Albert went to the shipping office. He was able to book a passage for his family. They would board a coastal trader within the week.

Chapter Two

1850 Hanging Rock

Robert toiled away in the heat of the spring day. Around him the recent rains were turning the landscape bright green with new growth and the wattle trees were a sea of bright yellow. His skin was tanned dark brown and his body had become hardened to the heavy work he performed every day. But it was lonely out here in the bush. He paused in his task of grubbing out yet another tree stump and leaned on his pick. As often happened lately, his thoughts went to his family, still living back in the old country.

The letter that he had hoped for had not arrived. He had written to his family months ago, but so far there had been no response. He felt a sense of despair as he wondered if his family had decided that they could not possibly join him. This was a harsh and inhospitable land. The days were hot in summer and could be freezing cold in winter and there were no comforts. Despite the hardships and privations of his life, he knew that his family could have a much better life here than they had all known in Wales. There was enough land so that each of his brothers could have a holding of their own.

The first years on the land had been kind to him. He had worked hard clearing the land, planting potatoes and tending to his sheep. Now his flock was growing. He watched the new baby lambs getting unsteadily to their feet and feeding from their mothers. The wool from his flock had fetched a good price. There had been steady rainfall and whilst the winters were cold, they had been reasonably mild. He had met other squatters and shepherds and was glad that he had arrived when he had. Things were changing. The government had begun to open up the land for sale. The times when men could just squat on land and run their sheep wherever they pleased were ending. He would eventually have to purchase his land if he was to keep it.

With a jerk, he brought his mind back to the present. Although he missed his family, he felt aggrieved and somewhat angry that he had not heard back from them, particularly given he had sent enough money to pay for their passages. He knew he must get a move on as today was muster day. He put his work aside, splashed water on his face from the trough and put on a clean shirt.

Robert saddled his horse. He knew that there would still be harsh frosts as the season moved into spring, but it was good to feel the sun on his back as he rode the few miles to Carlsruhe, where he was due to report for muster. He had been relieved to find that he did not have to travel to Melbourne each month for the muster, but rather he was able to report to the Police barracks in Carlsruhe.

Robert rode into the small settlement. The main buildings were the Carlsruhe station, the Inn and the police barracks. Robert tied his horse to the rail outside the barracks and was soon relieved to have that business completed for another month. Then he made his way to the Carlsruhe station from which the postal service was being run. Maybe the letter would be waiting for him today.

The Post Mistress greeted him with a smile. She was used to his visits and enquiries about a letter from Wales.

"You are in luck today, Mr. Blayney. Your letter has arrived."

Robert could not believe his ears. He took the letter, headed outside and tore it open. They were coming! What wonderful news! As he read on, he realised that, in fact, they might already be in Adelaide. The letter had probably arrived just ahead of them. He would need to make preparations to travel to Melbourne to meet them. Fortunately, he had prospered well enough to be able to hire a shepherd to help mind the sheep so he could leave him in charge for the few days it would take him to travel to Melbourne.

After all this time, their family would be together again.

1850 Port Phillip District

Robert haunted the Carlsruhe postal service over the following weeks until finally his mother's letter from Adelaide arrived. Preparations for the journey being already in place, he wasted no time in making his way to Melbourne to find his family. He hoped they had found somewhere to stay whilst they waited to hear from him. After enquiring at several hotels and lodging houses, he was reunited with them.

The family all milled around Robert as his mother embraced him. It was six long years since they had seen him.

"How are you, my son?" his mother asked, with tears glistening in her eyes. "It is so good to see you."

"I am fine," he replied, smiling at his father over his mother's shoulder, wondering if she would ever let him go so that he could greet his father and siblings.

"You look well, son," said his father, pumping his hand.

Robert greeted his brothers, Charles and George, and hugged Rebecca.

The reunion was sweet, made more so when Robert saw that his brother had brought his new wife with him. "This is my wife, Susannah," said George.

"It is a pleasure to meet you Susannah," said Robert, grinning at her. "But now we must get moving. We have quite a journey ahead before we get back to the farm."

Robert saw Albert and Harriet exchange a grim look. They both looked exhausted and there was still a long way to go. The family loaded their belongings into the cart and moved off, taking turns to ride in the cart and to walk alongside.

"I am glad that you managed to get a passage from Port Adelaide so quickly," said Robert to his mother, who sat beside him in the cart.

"The locals helped us to get tickets, and it was thankfully an uneventful journey," said Harriet. "This place is so busy. I thought Port Adelaide was busy, but it is nothing compared to Melbourne. There were so many ships of all shapes and sizes crowded into the harbour when we arrived. It is all new and daunting, but we have been lucky. People have been so ready to help us to find transport and lodgings here in Melbourne."

"I think it is incredibly exciting," said Charles as they travelled through the busy streets. Parts of the town were squalid, teeming with people living in all types of humpies and tents, but the newly laid out streets of central Melbourne were wide and quite a few imposing buildings already graced the town.

"You can almost smell the opportunities this place offers," said Charles. "I am glad that you have land Robert, but I can't help thinking it would be a fine idea to start a business here in town. I am sure I will be back."

Robert grinned at his brother, feeling a sense of pride that he had been instrumental in introducing his older brother to this exciting new life.

As they continued their journey, they soon left the town behind. The countryside was dotted with rough cottages where settlers had established small farms. Sheep grazed in the paddocks alongside cattle and a few horses. However, it was the wide-open spaces that astonished the Blayney family. They were used to small crowded allotments, but here there were vast tracts of pasture and heavily forested land with very little sign of habitation. The roads were still rough between Melbourne and their new home, so travel was slow and soon the newcomers were all exhausted. As the sun sank on the first day of their travels, they set up camp near a burbling creek and lit a fire. The sunset was glorious, glowing brightly with red and orange. Robert felt elated. Such a beautiful sunset must surely be a good omen. He had bought supplies and soon had the billy boiling for tea and the damper cooked. They were all famished by that point, so they tore pieces off the damper and ate hungrily. After they had eaten, Robert produced a flask from his pack and filled each of their pannikins with a tot of rum.

"Here's to new beginnings," said Robert in a toast to them all. He looked anxiously at his father, who was looking rather wan. But Albert raised his drink.

"Here, here," he said, and the family followed suit. "It has been a long and difficult journey and we are not there yet, but we hold out great hope, Robert."

Harriet took a small sip of her rum and smiled at Robert.

"You don't seem to be suffering too much from the effects of your imprisonment, Robert," she said.

"Well, I have had some time to recover, and hard work has made me strong. But it was not a good experience Mother," he replied. "The work we had to do was dreadfully monotonous. Day after day I sat amongst rows and rows of prisoners picking oakum, breaking apart the fibres of tarry old ropes that they used to fill gaps in the timbers of wooden ships. We were not allowed to talk. The prison guards stood over us, ready to pounce if we uttered even the smallest sound. We worked for eleven hours a day until our fingers bled."

Harriet flinched at this description.

"Oh Robert, that sounds dreadful."

"Yes, it was, and when we finally did get on board a ship, it didn't get much better. They packed us below decks with no more than the width of a body for each prisoner. And the stench was unbearable as we had no sanitary facilities. The only time we got a wash was when we were on deck for an hour each day. They hosed us down with freezing water. The drinking water went off, so they gave us a daily ration of rum, which was welcome of course, but didn't really help. We were still thirsty all the time. And hungry. We received the smallest of rations which were barely edible. Many died on the journey."

"How did you get your ticket of leave after you had only served two years of your sentence?" asked his brother Charles, interested in practicalities rather than descriptions of Robert's deprivations.

"We arrived here in Port Phillip, thinking we had actually landed in Van Diemen's Land. The ship's captain announced that we were to be issued with a ticket of leave. I could not believe it. Apparently, the reason was that they needed labourers and shepherds so desperately that they would take a chance on convicts."

By this time, everyone was yawning. It had been a long and difficult day. They settled themselves on the hard ground as best they could to try to get some rest.

As the others dozed off, Robert sat gazing at the dying embers of the campfire and wondered whether he had done the right thing convincing his family to join him. Would they be able to adapt to the conditions? He had made his way well enough, but would they? He had been in terrible shape, half starved, when he had arrived, yet he had managed to get on with it and start to build a future for them all. His thoughts drifted to all he had been through since he had set foot on the banks of the Yarra River four years earlier.

Chapter Three

1846 Melbourne

The prisoners took up the oars of the longboat and rowed past Batman Hill up the Yarra River. Robert breathed in the fresh air. Unfamiliar odours assailed his senses. He would soon learn that one of the main scents was that of the eucalypts, those strange-looking trees that filled so much of the landscape. He had never seen the likes of these trees before. But he knew much about this strange new land would be foreign to him. He and the other prisoners landed on the banks of the Yarra, just below a waterfall. He stumbled out of the longboat, unsteady on his feet after so long at sea and surveyed his surroundings, wondering what would happen next. Suddenly, it dawned that it depended solely on him, but it had been so long since he had known freedom. Robert had no idea what to do.

He made his way into the streets of the new town of Melbourne, a town that was now just four years old. His eyes were drawn to John Batman's home, which was the most prominent building, perched on Batman's Hill overlooking the river.

The sun was low in the sky, a fiery ball on the horizon. The heat was intense even this late in the day. Robert decided to head back to the river and find a spot where he could spend the night. He removed his boots and waded into the river and splashed water over his head. The water was chilly, but he felt refreshed as he tried to remove some of the grime that had built up over the months at sea. He grabbed a handful of sand from the riverbank and scrubbed his face and hands. Tomorrow, when the sun came up, he promised himself he would rinse his shirt. As usual, he was starving, so he ate a small portion of the dry bread from the meagre rations that had been provided to all the prisoners as they left the ship. He wondered at the tea and sugar as he had no means to boil water. As he ate, he watched the water birds feeding in the shallows of the river or with their wings outspread making the most of the last of the day's sun. He arranged his sack of belongings as a pillow and settled down to sleep. The sky darkened around him and he was thankful for the warm night, as he had no blanket.

The next morning, Robert rinsed his shirt and washed in the river again, then waited for his shirt to dry. Today he hoped to make the acquaintance of someone who might provide him with a meal in exchange for some odd jobs.

Robert walked up towards the town again. As midday approached he found himself at the Old Governor Hotel. As he entered the crowded hotel, heads turned. Although Robert had tried to clean himself up, he knew he must still look dirty and unkempt, and he did not feel particularly welcome as he scanned the unfriendly faces. He supposed they would all know that a convict ship had entered the harbour and discharged a full complement of prisoners. He wondered whether anyone would welcome them.

"Are you one of those Penton Villains?" said a man sitting at the bar.

"I don't know what you mean," replied Robert, determined to stay calm and keep his temper in check.

"Don't think you are the first lot of convicts who have landed here as free men. Have you served your full sentence?"

"That is really none of your business," retorted Robert, his face growing hot. He was naturally quick-tempered but did not want to make enemies in his first hours here.

"You are not welcome here. We are a law-abiding lot, and we don't need the likes of you."

"I hear differently," Robert replied. "Apparently there are plenty of people who need strong, healthy men to work for them." Fortunately, apart from a final scornful look in Robert's direction, the man took the matter no further. Robert felt his rising temper abate.

Despite the initial lack of hospitality, Robert struck up a conversation with the bartender.

"Do you have any odd jobs that I could do? All I would ask in return is a meal and a tankard of ale."

The bartender was a kindly man and set Robert the task of stacking crates and removing rubbish to the rear of the hotel. Soon enough, he had earned a meal of lamb stew with bread and a tankard of fine English Ale. After surviving on prison rations for such a long time, he soon felt full and struggled to finish the meal. Nevertheless, the food and alcohol tasted like freedom. He could not remember the last time he had been able to fill his belly until he felt sated. After he completed his meal, he again spoke to the bartender.

"Do you know where I could get some work?" he asked.

"What do you do?" asked the bartender.

"I was a farmer back home."

"Where's that?"

"Wales."

"I tell you, if I had a quid or two, I wouldn't be working for another man."

"What do you mean?"

"I'd get me a flock of sheep and head out of town."

"Really? Could I do that?" Robert asked again. He was not used to such freedoms.

"There is land out there for the taking. Build a fence and a hut and it's yours, basically."

This information caused Robert to draw breath. Land for the taking. It seemed impossible. He thanked the bartender and went off to explore the settlement, turning over this new information in his mind. He walked towards the market and wandered through the rows of carts stacked with all types of produce being sold by local market gardeners. Also, for sale were a great variety of wares, tools, cooking utensils, poultry and eggs, suckling pigs and rabbits, to name a few. The streets were wide but filled with the rank stench of people and animals living closely huddled together.

Robert needed to make some money fast. It was the dream of any farmer to own his own piece of land. To think that here in this new colony, he could become the landholder, master of his own destiny. His mind was brimming with the possibilities.

He approached a man with a cart laden with all manner of tools and gear.

"Hello there," he said, "I have just arrived in Melbourne. I am looking for work."

"Welcome to Melbourne," said the trader in a strong Welsh accent. "Sounds like we are from the same neck of the woods. Where in Wales are you from?"

"Yes, you are right. I am also a Welshman. I am from Beguildy," said Robert. "How long have you been here?"

"A little over a year. I am just starting to find my feet now. There is plenty of work around."

"It is great to meet a fellow countryman," said Robert, and the two men shook hands. "Who should I talk to about some work?"

"There is a landholder not far from here who is looking for a labourer to help build fences on his sheep property."

"Alright, thank you for your help," said Robert.

Following the stallholders' directions, Robert made his way to the property and looked around until he found the owner.

"Do you need a willing worker?" he asked.

"What can you do?" asked the landholder.

"What do you need? I am strong and fit, and I can turn my hand to anything."

"Have you ever sawn timber?"

"No, but I am sure I can learn."

"Well, get to work then. See Martin over there in the sawpit and he will show you the ropes."

It was hard work cutting down the enormous trees and sawing them into slabs to make the post and rail fences. He and another man worked in partnership. Robert, being the least experienced of the pair, worked down in the sawpit, whilst his partner worked above ground. The pit saw moved back and forward between them, with sawdust constantly raining down on him. It was hard work in the ferociously hot summer.

Robert could purchase everything he needed at the nearby market and was soon able to set up a modest camp with his own tent and cooking fire. He was quickly learning the ways of the settlers, making billy tea and stew and damper in his camp oven. Mutton was plentiful, as were potatoes and some vegetables, so he ate well for the first time in his life.

After several months, Robert was in a position to go off on his own to explore the countryside that was opening up around him and hopefully find his own piece of land. He told the landholder of his decision to move on.

"Where are you off to?" asked the landholder.

"That I am not really sure about, but I have heard plenty about excellent farming land to be had," replied Robert.

"I have been told there is suitable land around Mount Macedon and a place called Hanging Rock. Seems you need to travel northwest over Mt. Macedon and through the Black

Forest. But watch out for the local Aboriginal People. I hear they can be aggressive out in the bush."

Robert thanked the landholder for hiring him and set off to make final preparations. Although he was new to this strange land, he felt confident that he had learned enough to survive in the interior. He made his way back to his Welsh friend at the market to purchase the tools he now knew he would need. His final purchase was a sturdy horse which would carry him and his supplies into the unknown.

1847 The Interior of Port Phillip District

It was a long and arduous journey. The terrain was rugged, and the tracks were rough and unmade. Robert wondered at the tracks, though. They crisscrossed each other, and many were well worn. Surely there had not been that many people wandering around in this harsh interior to make such tracks. Perhaps they were made by animals. He had seen some small groups of the local Aboriginal People, so he knew they inhabited these parts. Was it possible that all these tracks were made by these people?

Robert continued his trek through the bush of towering gums and stubbly undergrowth. He saw many strange-looking animals as he traveled. Kangaroos munched quietly on green shoots of grass. He saw wombats who disappeared into their burrows as they saw him approach. Goannas scurried up tree trunks, causing Robert to look up and see koalas in the tops of the gums along with many species of birds. He came to an area of thick dark bush which rose over the range. He guessed this might be the Black Forest and once he made his way through, he might be getting close to the land that had been described to him. The trek through the forest was daunting. His horse shied more than once at the shadows under the thick dark canopy of the ancient gum trees.

After several days, he arrived at a homestead. It was a primitive dwelling made from timber with a bark roof. But it was substantial, and the land around had been cleared and fences had been erected to make paddocks for a large flock of sheep. There was a cow in another enclosure near a small shed and another outbuilding.

He made his way to the front of the homestead and called out.

"Hello, is anybody there?" said Robert.

A pretty but harried looking young woman came to the door. Long hours in the sun had tanned her face and arms. Robert thought she seemed a little uncertain at his sudden appearance. It was probably unusual for strangers to show up at her door.

"How do you do ma'am, I don't mean you any harm," said Robert. "I have just ridden from Melbourne. It is good to see a sign of life. May I ask who lives here?"

"I am Esther, and my husband farms this land. He is out at work with the sheep at present."

"What do you farm here?"

"Well, we have our sheep and we have also planted some potatoes. Would you like a cup of tea?"

"Thank you," said Robert. "That would be very much appreciated."

Esther directed Robert to a seat on the verandah where it was cooler and went inside to prepare the tea. She soon appeared again with a tray laden with a china pot of tea with delicate cups and saucers and scones with cream and jam. He had a feeling that she was pleased to have some company for a while.

As they sat on the verandah drinking the welcome cup of tea, Esther shared more information about the farm.

"The soil is rich, and rainfall is generally good. But we have been through some dry years. I grow vegetables in a small plot at the back. So, we usually have enough to eat at least. But it is hard out here."

Robert saw a rider approaching.

"Ah, here is my husband," said Esther.

She rose to get a cup for her husband whilst Robert introduced himself to the sunburned squatter, whose name, it transpired, was Benjamin.

"It is good to meet you, Benjamin," said Robert.

"It is good to meet you too," replied Benjamin, throwing his dusty hat down onto a spare chair. "It is rather a lonely life out here. We don't get many visitors." He was a tall, good-looking man, with a certain strength about him. And it was obvious that he doted on his wife. She smiled at him as she poured him a cup of tea and passed him a scone from the tray.

"As I told your wife, I have just traveled from Melbourne hoping to find some land on which to start a farm. I was hoping you might have some work available," said Robert. "I don't have any stock yet and need to earn enough to buy some sheep."

"Yes, as a matter of fact, there is plenty of work around these parts at the moment," replied Benjamin. "We need another shepherd to look after the sheep."

"Well, that suits me just fine," said Robert. "I have not long arrived from Wales where my family were sheep farmers, so that is definitely something that I can do."

So, it was decided. Benjamin showed Robert the male servants' quarters, which was a comparatively comfortable two-roomed hut built in the same fashion as the main homestead. There was one other shepherd who would share the accommodation. Then Benjamin invited Robert to join him and Esther for dinner.

Esther served a delicious meal of roast mutton with vegetables. Robert salivated as he caught the aroma. He had eaten little more than damper and billy tea for some time, so enjoyed the meal immensely.

"Thank you, Esther, that was a marvellous meal," he said, as Esther cleared away the dishes. The two men sat in companionable silence and enjoyed a tot of rum before turning in.

The next day, Robert met the other shepherd who showed him around the farm. He was directed to a substantial flock of sheep, which he took charge of. He herded the sheep in the surrounding pastures so that they could feed on new grass each day. At the end of each day, he rounded the sheep up and if they were close enough to the homestead, he would return them to the paddock. Other nights, he camped out with the sheep when the availability of pasture meant that they had to be some distance from the homestead. The nights were bitter as the season moved into winter. Many a morning would see him waken to a white frost. One morning, after he had shivered in his bed, he woke to see snow on Mt Macedon. Despite his discomfort the cooler weather was somehow familiar and comforting. He had not yet become accustomed to the extreme heat of the Port Phillip summers.

Robert worked for Benjamin for some time, but he had bigger plans and soon grew restless. He decided it was time to move on. He approached Benjamin with the news.

"I want to thank you for giving me work, Benjamin," said Robert. "But it is time for me to move on. Would you sell me some sheep to start my flock?"

By now, the two men had become friends, so Benjamin readily agreed to sell Robert the sheep. Before he left, he also stocked up on flour, tea and sugar from the stores at the farmhouse. Esther was keen to help in any way she could, so she was happy to sell him these staples. He also bought some potatoes as he had seen Benjamin harvest a good crop, so he planned to try his own planting. Robert thanked Benjamin and Esther and went on his way.

That night, he camped on the banks of a nearby creek. The following morning, he rounded up his small flock of sheep. The pasture was good, so the sheep had grazed quietly overnight and had not wandered far.

1847 Hanging Rock

Robert traveled for another full day until what he suspected was Hanging Rock came into view. Benjamin and Esther had described the mysterious outcrop which seemed to appear from nowhere out of the surrounding plains. He stared in amazement. He could see that there were acres of grassland, but also plenty of timbered areas.

The outcrop itself was like no hill or mountain he had ever seen before. Robert had heard stories about how the huge granite monolith had formed many thousands of years ago when the molten lava had bubbled up from the ground in a mighty volcanic eruption. Robert turned his horse towards the rock. He soon found that icy cold spring water flowed from the base of the rock into a creek. He peered up at the towering columns of rock. Vegetation and smaller trees clung to the sides of the formation, poking out at strange angles, as if at any moment they might topple over. Surprisingly, in this diverse landscape, there was a lack of colour, just the grey of the rock and the dull, dark green of the lichen, the ferns, the moss and the gums. On this day of Robert's arrival, the heat was oppressive and enhanced the scent emanating from the eucalypts. It reminded Robert of when he had first set foot in Port Phillip.

Everywhere around the rock Robert could hear birds among the leaves of the tall eucalypts. He heard the shrill sound of great flocks of cockatoos as they screeched over-head. As the cockatoos moved away into the distance, he could hear the more pleasant sound of well-hidden bellbirds, like a chorus of tiny bells chiming in the wind. He also spot-ted more kangaroos munching lazily on fresh shoots of grass and koalas perched in the manna gums, chewing away at the leaves. By now, he was becoming more familiar with this strange wildlife.

Robert was pleased with everything he saw. He knew that a constant source of water would be critical, as both he and his newly acquired livestock would not survive without it. As he explored the land, he found the creek seemed to flow steadily, even though summer was approaching and rainfall had been scant over the cold winter months. Robert knelt on one knee and scooped up some water in his cupped hand. The water was clear and tasted good despite its reddish tinge. Once he had satisfied his thirst, he looked around him further.

He found a spot to set up camp, not far from the creek bank. He cut some stout branches from a nearby gum sapling to make a framework for his tent, threw the canvas over and pegged it to the ground. This would be his home until he could build a more substantial dwelling. He wondered at his chances of catching a fish in the creek to supplement his meal and soon found that fish were plentiful. Once he had caught enough for his dinner, he lit a fire and settled the billy to boil and got a damper underway. He grilled the fish over the hot coals. He was proud of his newfound cooking skills and was pleased that he had also learned how to fish whilst in Benjamin's employ. It was a delicious meal and Robert felt like a king.

Robert was not entirely sure how to stake his claim to this land, but he thought he would just mark some trees with his axe and see if anyone objected. Apparently, this was what others had done. He had seen the evidence on trees as he made his way here. But he had not seen anything for some time, so he supposed he could claim this land.

As the shadows lengthened and darkness fell, he could see the eyes of possums shining in the trees by the light of his campfire. Suddenly, he heard a strange droning sound emanating from the thick bush nearby. With fear rising in his belly, he hesitantly moved towards the sound. He was not sure he wanted to know what it was, but he felt he must find out for his own safety. As he crept through the thick bush, he smelt smoke and soon saw a large fire burning in a clearing. Big strong looking Aboriginal men danced naked around the fire. They had decorated their bodies with patterns painted with what looked to Robert like mud. A group of women sat to the side, tapping sticks in unison with the stamping feet of the dancing men. Fear stirred in Robert as he watched on. He was all alone out here in the bush and had not seen another white man since he had left Benjamin's property. He crept back to his camp and lay sleepless for a long time wondering whether the people he had seen earlier would attack him in his bed.

Despite his anxiety, Robert eventually drifted off to sleep. The next morning, he awoke as the sun rose. All around him were huge gums that had stood for centuries. The early morning light filtered onto the trunks and leaves, turning them golden and silver where the sun could reach, whilst other parts remained shaded, grey and colourless. However, he was still feeling unsettled, so he again crept to the scene of the gathering and saw that the Aboriginal People were gone. The only evidence of the night's activities was the dead campfire. Robert wondered whether this was indeed a good place to settle, but soon decided he had to take his chances. The local Aboriginal People were a mysterious and ominous presence. He had heard that they had stolen sheep from other landholders. But according to Benjamin, they hadn't caused his family any trouble and Robert had been out here for some time and had not come to any harm so far.

Once he had investigated the scene of last night's gathering, Robert started work on his new land. After a meal of the previous night's leftover damper and billy tea laced with plenty of sugar, he set to work. By now, he was adept at cutting down trees and using the timber to build fences. Although he didn't have a partner or a saw pit, he had also learned to use his maul and wedge to split the logs into reasonable rails. He started with a small paddock for his sheep. He dug holes for the posts after cutting slots for the rails to fit snugly into. Then he started work on his hut. He cut down some more of the surrounding trees to clear a larger area and used this timber to cut the slabs for his one-roomed hut. He stripped the bark from the trees and used that for the roof. The new dwelling was very rough, but he felt more secure, and it provided better shelter than a tent.

It was hard work in the heat of early summer, but he was pleased with the efforts of his first weeks on his new land. He now had an acceptable dwelling, and his sheep were fenced in and had plenty of pasture on which to feed.

Chapter Four

1850 Hanging Rock

The Blayney family were all relieved that the interminable journey was finally over when Robert's humble property came into view. Still, Harriet could tell that the newly arrived family were apprehensive at what lay ahead for them in this new environment. She tried to show her enthusiasm as Robert proudly showed them the progress he had made. He took them on a tour of his land and showed them his hut. He pointed out Hanging Rock and told his family of the springs at the base that fed the creek. His sheep were grazing quietly on the pasture in the paddock and his most recent acquisition, a cow, stood swishing flies with its tail. There was another crop of potatoes almost ready for harvest.

It was an unbearably hot day and the flies swarmed around the family in droves. Harriet was daunted by all that confronted them. She was exhausted after the journey and she was anxious about Albert, who she knew had found the long journey particularly difficult. The young people seemed to be more optimistic. Harriet knew they would see the opportunities that would open up to them in this new land.

"How much land have you claimed, Robert?" asked Charles.

"There is plenty for us to each have a piece," said Robert. "We will need to build more huts so we can all have a place of our own. And we can make allowance for Michael when he is able to join us."

The family fell silent as they thought about Michael. As far as they knew, he was currently serving 10 years in the brutal penal colony of Van Diemen's Land. They had heard nothing from him and Harriet hoped he was indeed still alive and had not succumbed to the brutality of the system.

"I was granted a ticket of leave in under two years," said Robert. "So, if he is keeping his nose clean, he should soon be granted his freedom as well. In the meantime, we can get a piece of land in each of our names."

Rebecca had moved quietly away from the family. Despite her own uncertainty, Harriet noticed Rebecca seemed unsettled and joined her out of earshot of the others.

"What is the matter, Rebecca?" Harriet asked.

"It is all very well for the boys," she answered. "They will all have their land. My prospects are limited in this lonely place."

"My hope for you is that you might find a husband here where there are better opportunities for all of us," said her mother.

Rebecca sighed.

"That seems rather unlikely at the moment, Mother. There doesn't seem to be anyone around for miles."

Harriet left Rebecca to her thoughts and moved back to Albert's side. She looked at Charles, wondering what he was thinking. She knew Charles saw himself as the most likely to succeed. As the oldest brother, he had always been the leader of the four boys. But unlike Michael and Robert, he had managed to keep out of reach of the law in the old country. She knew that he had been involved in some rather shady business trying to beat the greedy landlords. He had just never been caught, which meant he did not share the convict taint of his brothers.

George and Susannah had not said anything until now. George was the quiet member of the family. He had worked hard and kept out of trouble. But now Harriet heard him talking quietly to Susannah.

"What do you think, Susannah?" he asked his new wife.

"Oh, my George," she replied. "I am quite in shock. This place is rather mysterious, is it not? Nevertheless, I am sure we will have a grand adventure here."

George smiled broadly. Harriet was pleased to hear that Susannah seemed to share George's sense of excitement at what the future might hold. She knew how proud George was of the bravery his wife had shown since he convinced her to marry him and come away on this adventure. She had been seriously ill on the voyage and they had all feared that, like so many others who had died on the ship, she might not make it. But as the ship's surgeon had foreseen, once they disembarked, she had recovered quickly.

The family went about setting up their four farms — one for each of Albert and Harriet's sons. Albert and Harriet would help the boys and would make their home on the piece of land being saved for when Michael became a free man. Rebecca would live with her parents as long as she remained single.

Together they worked to clear more land, using the timber to commence building three more huts. They worked the land and helped Robert to harvest his potatoes and shear his sheep. Harriet, Rebecca and Susannah cultivated a garden to grow vegetables to help feed the family. With the proceeds of the potato crop and another good wool sale, they were able to purchase turkeys and chickens to provide eggs and another cow for milk and butter. These were long, hard days of backbreaking work in the increasing heat as the year drew to a close.

Their first Christmas in Port Phillip was quite an occasion. It was a scorchingly hot day and Harriet wondered how they would enjoy the day in the face of such oppressive heat.

She stood by the fire, fanning herself with a cloth.

"Oh, it is so hot, Albert," she moaned.

"That it is lass," replied Albert. "How is our Christmas dinner coming along?"

"I may faint from heat exhaustion before I get it cooked."

Their mouths watered as they smelt the turkey roasting with the vegetables in the pots hung over the open fire.

"This is so different to back home," said Harriet. She missed the cold at this time of the year. And in this festive season, she was feeling homesick. She couldn't help wondering how family and friends they had left behind were faring.

"Very different, but not worse," said Albert. "I know you miss the old country but think of the advantages we have already found here. Back home we would have been huddled around a fire with not enough to eat, let alone able to make it a celebration. Today we get to fill our stomachs with delicious turkey, and there will be plenty for everyone."

Gradually all the family assembled around the table of Albert and Harriet's home, wishing each other Happy Christmas. They had decorated the rough slab hut with mistletoe and flowering gum. They did not have a fir tree as they would have had back home, but they had made do with a branch from a eucalypt tree gaily decorated with bright homemade paper ornaments. Under the tree, there were seven small gifts wrapped in brown paper and string. One for each of them.

They all sat down around the table as Harriet dished up the meal.

Robert poured each of them a tot of rum, then raised his pannikin.

"Here's to our first Christmas at Hanging Rock."

They all joined Robert in the toast and enjoyed the delicious meal topped off with a serving of Harriet's delicious suet pudding served with custard. It was a happy Christmas.

Fortunately, the weather had been kind since they had arrived. Things changed quickly, however, and as the summer set in and temperatures rose, they came to understand how harsh the land could be. Soon after Christmas, the hot dry weather really started to take its toll. Their good start to life in Port Phillip was not to last.

1851 Hanging Rock Black Thursday

The sun beat down relentlessly on the scorched earth. There had not been a drop of rain for months, and everywhere the ground was parched and dry, baked hard by the sun. Drought gripped the state and the springs and creeks that had flowed so well started to dry up. The creek beds were merely mud in some parts and in others they had dried completely, leaving criss-crossed cracks in the mud.

Harriet looked over the land and their livestock in despair. The countryside was bare of pasture and the sheep were starving. Fortunately, the family had been able to purchase feed for the sheep, but they did not know how much longer they could afford this luxury. They knew that many other farmers in the surrounding district were watching their sheep dying in the paddocks and Harriet wondered how long it would be before their own sheep died. Each day, the situation deteriorated. But then came the worst day of all.

Albert and Harriet sat in the shade of the verandah of the home that they had helped their sons to build. It was the coolest place they could find.

"It is already unbearably hot and not yet midday," Harriet said to Albert, fanning herself with her newspaper. Albert stood and looked at the horizon.

"Can you smell smoke?" he asked. They had seen smoke intermittently rising in the surrounding ranges for weeks now. The shepherds had told them that the smoke was from campfires that foolhardy workers passing through hadn't extinguished properly. They wondered why people were so careless in the tinder dry bush. But until now, the fires had not been close to home.

"Oh dear lord, no. If there is a fire today, nothing will stop it," replied Harriet.

Even as newcomers to the Port Phillip district, they were beginning to understand that bush fires would be a constant danger during the hot, dry summer months.

They continued to survey the surrounding horizon, and soon they noticed smoke rising to the south from the Black Forest. There was a howling wind, searingly hot, blowing from the northwest. They watched transfixed, as nearby Mount Macedon suddenly erupted in flames. The intense heat increased. Albert and Harriet felt like their lungs were collapsing. The acrid smell of smoke became overwhelming, irritating their eyes and throat.

"Oh Albert, where are the boys? We must let them know, make sure they are safe," said Harriet.

But just as she uttered these words, Robert and Charles came running up to their parents' cottage.

"The fire is burning out of control," cried Charles. "We need to get the sheep into the home paddock as quickly as possible in case the wind changes. You should go to the creek and take shelter. Where is Rebecca? Take woollen blankets with you. We will check on George and Susannah."

"I'll come with you," said Albert.

"No Father," said Robert, "No need. You would do better to look after the womenfolk."

Harriet was relieved. She knew Albert would also be relieved to be able to join the women at the creek. He was not moving as well as he would have liked. His joints were becoming stiffer and more painful by the day.

Harriet watched anxiously as the two boys ran off to George's home and soon Susannah had joined Albert, Harriet and Rebecca, gathering up blankets and heading to the creek. Harriet prayed silently that her boys would be careful and not get hurt.

All the time, the fire was increasing in intensity giving the sky a strange orange glow and blanketing the entire district with thick black smoke. Albert and the womenfolk huddled together in water up to their waists. They were fortunate that at least this deep hole in the creek still contained some water.

Harriet felt her fear rising as they watched the scene unfold. From the safety of the creek, they watched the fire progress. The direction of the wind was blowing the fire to the west of their property, so they could only hope that the worst of it might pass them by. Even so, the wind could change at any time. The flames must have been hundreds of feet high as they came roaring through the Black Forest and over Mount Macedon, igniting every twig and blade of grass in their path. The skies filled with walls of red and yellow flames and pillars of smoke blocked out the sun. Suffocating smoke and the rank smell of burning were almost unbearable. Albert and the women in the creek tied wet cloths over their mouths and noses, hoping for some small protection against the smoke and heat.

Albert tried to reassure the women.

"The boys will be alright, they are all young and strong. They will take cover if they need to."

"I am not so sure, Albert," said Harriet. "They have no experience of fire. I don't know that they will know when to take cover. They will be so determined to protect our land and animals."

After several hours, they could see that the fire had burned its way past their properties, leaving a blackened but still glowing path behind it. Huge old gum trees smoldered, glowing red and smoking.

"Do you think it is safe to go back home now, Albert?" said Harriet. "I am so worried about the boys."

"Yes, I think if we go carefully, we will be safe enough," replied Albert. As they waded out of the creek and moved slowly through the still smoldering debris, they could see that the worst of the fire had burned to the west of their property as they had hoped it would.

They found the boys, blackened with soot, thirsty and exhausted.

"Oh, thank goodness you are safe," exclaimed Harriet, hugging each of the boys in turn.

"We are fine mother," said Charles, struggling to talk, his breath faltering. "I can taste smoke and ash and my lungs are still burning, which is making it hard to catch my breath, but otherwise I am fine." Robert and George nodded their agreement.

"Where are all the stock?" asked Albert.

The boys related how they had struggled to round up the skittish sheep.

"They ran around in circles because they smelt the smoke," said Robert. "We eventually mustered them into the paddock closest to the creek and then led the cow and the horses into the same paddock. We hoped the animals would be sensible enough to take shelter in the water. We just turned the chickens and turkeys out of their enclosures and hoped they could take care of themselves and escape the flames."

Charles continued the story as Robert was racked by a fit of coughing.

"Once we had taken care of the livestock, we just did what we could to protect our properties. We removed as much flammable material as possible from around the cottages, hoping to create something of a firebreak. Then we stood guard, using green branches and wet sacking to put out any spot fires that started from flying embers. It certainly was a close call. I hope we never have to go through that again."

As the catastrophic day drew to a close and the temperature dropped slightly, the family took stock. They surely were some of the lucky ones. The fire had burned close to their property but had damaged nothing. They knew the fate of their neighbours would be much worse. They went to check on the sheep and found that they were safe. As were the cows and Robert's two horses. The chickens and turkeys soon returned to their roosts.

The fires continued to burn for the rest of the week despite the cooler temperatures and the wind swinging around to the south. Eventually, they burnt themselves out.

The newspapers over the days and weeks that followed told an horrific tale. There had been a series of fires right across the Port Phillip District that day.

The decimation of Mount Macedon was clear to see, but the newspapers reported that the fire had burned the whole of Fitzroy town, leaving only brick chimneys standing. One evening, Harriet sat at the table and the family gathered around as she read the reports out loud.

The scorching winds and the tinder dry undergrowth caused by the excessively dry summer provided the perfect ingredients for this disaster. Lives have been lost and thousands of sheep and cattle, as well as native animals, have perished. Great tracts of land have burned, from the Plenty Ranges to

Geelong, then across Mount Macedon and through the Black Forest and on to the South Australian border. At Cape Otway, the dense forest of eucalypts and the undergrowth exploded as nobody would ever have imagined. Normally, a fire would burn slowly in such a thickly forested place. Many timber cutters lost their livelihoods as their stockpiles of timber burned.

Harriet read about the German settlers around Geelong who, like the Blayneys, had only been in the Port Phillip District for a year.

"They have lost everything," Harriet told her family. "All the plants they had grown from seed and the grapevines they had brought with them have been burned to the ground. To think that they nursed all those plants through the long voyage to Port Phillip and now they are all gone. Fortunately, the fire spared their homes, although I can't imagine how."

The Blayney family were indeed lucky to come through with no loss of life or stock. The hot summer drew on until at long last the weather started to cool and there was some decent rainfall. Harriet watched as the land came back to life. Huge old gum trees that had been reduced to smoldering trunks soon had new growth appearing along their entire length. The ground sprouted with shoots of grass, spreading a bright green carpet over the countryside. The family was able to get on with their lives and continue to build the farms and increase their flocks of sheep. Harriet felt grateful that despite the monumental disaster, the land could quickly recover with some cooling rain.

Then one day in July, Robert burst into his mother's kitchen.

Chapter Five

1851 Mt Alexander Goldfields

"Have you heard the news, Mother?" said an excited Robert, removing his hat as he entered the cottage. The timber slab hut had seen some improvements over the last year. It now had a stone fireplace and chimney so that they could heat their home and cook over the open fire rather than outside over a campfire. Harriet was cooking a mutton stew for herself, Albert and Rebecca.

"No Robert, I haven't," replied his ever patient and unflappable mother. She was dressed in simple garb, a green and brown plaid patterned cotton dress which served her well enough for daytime on the farm. Her buttoned boots peeked out from beneath her dress.

"It's gold. They've discovered gold."

Robert was instantly aware of his mother's apprehension at this announcement.

"It is just down the road at Mount Alexander," he said. "I have to take my chance to make us rich."

"Oh, Robert, please don't make a hasty decision," said his mother. "We are just finding our feet. If you go off to the goldfields, the rest of us will have to keep the farms going. And you know your father is not as strong as he used to be."

Robert was thoughtful for a moment. He knew he was taking a risk. They were all settling in well. The land they farmed was rich and, despite the dry summer, they had kept most of their flock of sheep alive. The autumn and winter rains had been good so far and they all hoped for a better season in the coming spring. The sheep were now looking well and would yield a good quantity of wool and many of the ewes had mated and would be lambing soon.

He looked out of the square opening in the wall of the cottage which served as a window. Glass was scarce. They covered the windows with woven pieces of wattle branches when they needed to keep the weather out. He could see the sheep, fenced in with good solid post and rail fencing. They had all worked extremely hard in the year since the family had arrived. But despite the risk, he was determined to go.

"It will be alright, Mother. I will only be gone a month or so, you'll see. It is very early in the rush and they say they are picking up nuggets off the ground."

"Well, I doubt that, but I see I cannot convince you to change your mind."

Robert discussed his plans with Charles. He knew Charles wanted to set up business in Melbourne, but Robert was keen to ensure that Charles would take care of the farms whilst he was away.

"Well, brother, I envy your sense of adventure," said Charles in response to Robert's request. "And I wish you luck. I hope you can make your fortune."

"Charles, I have no doubt that I will come back with enough gold for all of us so we can continue to build up our stock."

"Well, I hope so, Robert, but I would prefer to take my chances with something less reliant on luck."

Robert frowned, not at all pleased at his brother's lack of enthusiasm for his plans.

"Look," said Charles, "I understand this is an opportunity of sorts. You should go. We can manage the farms for a couple of months. Just don't be gone too long."

Robert refused to be deterred by his brother's lack of faith and began his preparations. He got together his kit of gold pan, pick and shovel, swag and cooking utensils.

On a cold and cloudy July morning, the family gathered to farewell him as he started out on his journey. He had to travel on foot because they would need the horses to work the farm whilst he was away. He had purchased a new wheelbarrow to carry his supplies.

The road was crowded with folk from every walk of life. Families in drays laden with everything they owned. Single men with just what they could carry in swags on their backs. Some, like Robert, pushed wheelbarrows. The winter rain had made the rough bush tracks boggy and the passage of so many carts, drays and wheelbarrows had left them hopelessly rutted and almost impassable. Robert was thankful that he hadn't far to go. The Mount Alexander goldfields were close to home. He hoped to walk the distance in 3 or 4 days.

The walk to the Goldfields was difficult and as he trudged on Robert saw more than one vehicle hopelessly bogged up to the axles. Beasts and men struggled together to pull them out of the sucking mud. Eventually, Robert made it to the diggings.

Although he was one of the early arrivals, the goldfields were already crowded. He stared around him at the mounds of dirt which covered the landscape with the creek flowing through the middle. Everywhere men were feverishly working their claims. The scene reminded him of an anthill.

Robert first had to stake his claim. He surveyed his surroundings and spoke to several of the men who were already well into the business of prospecting for gold.

"Good day there," he said to one particularly prosperous looking miner. "Have you had any luck?"

"I am doing alright," said the miner.

"Do you have any suggestions where I should stake my claim?" Robert asked.

"Your guess is as good as mine. There's no way of telling. Some blokes have struck it rich, discovering big nuggets, yet all around them other blokes strike out day after day."

Armed with this information, Robert went to the gold office and purchased his miner's license. It cost him 20 shillings, which was a huge amount of money — close to a week's wage. And this would only last him a month. But he would not risk the police catching him without one. He had heard that some diggers objected to being forced to have a license, so they kept a lookout and would warn each other when the troopers were around so they could go to ground. The ever-optimistic Robert felt sure he could make his fortune in less than a month before his licence ran out and return to his family with all the money they needed to continue to farm the land and to buy some thoroughbred horses. He had a powerful love of horses and thought that if he could make a go of it here, he could start a breeding program. He wasn't that keen on the idea of grubbing potatoes and chasing sheep around for the rest of his life.

He found a likely-looking piece of land by the creek on which to stake his claim and set up his camp. His shiny new gold pan glimmered in the bright sunlight as he filled it with sand from the creek bed for the first time. He added some water and started swilling, gradually washing the sand away. As he reached the dregs of the sand, he peered into the pan, looking for the telltale golden colour which, if he was lucky, would be trapped in the rim of the pan.

Although he worked very hard that first day, he was not rewarded. He did not see one speck of gold in his pan. At dusk, he took himself off to one of the sly grog shanties and bought himself a bottle of rum. Not wanting company after the long, tiring day, he took his bottle back to his camp and sat drinking morosely.

The next day, he rose with a headache. He headed down to the creek and sluiced water all over himself. Hangover or not, he could not afford to waste time and so after a breakfast of damper and black tea, he began work again.

This routine continued for several days and by the end of a week, when he still had had no luck, he was beginning to think he had set himself on a fool's mission. Every day he saw others shouting with glee as they struck gold on their claims. But he had nothing. Not one grain. Maybe his claim was worthless. All around him, though, men were finding gold. Surely he would have some luck soon.

He had struck up a friendship with the miner who was working a claim immediately to the east of him. The miner had been a city dweller before seeking his fortune and was struggling with the harsh conditions of the goldfields. Robert felt sorry for him and helped where he could. They shared the odd bottle of rum on occasion. Like Robert, his neighbour had had very little luck so far. Then one early morning, as Robert started work on his claim, his neighbour gave a shout.

"At last!" he yelled and waved his hand above his head.

"What is it?" said Robert as he wandered over to his friend.

"Have a look at this," he said and opened his fist to disclose a nugget the size of a small egg.

"That looks a good size. It should be worth a bit," said Robert. "If only my luck would change. I have not found even the smallest grain."

But still, his luck did not change.

One evening, after a long hard day, Robert was close to despair. He met his friend coming back to his tent.

"What do you say to a drink, my friend?" asked Robert. "I need to drown my sorrows."

The two men headed towards a newly established hotel, which was by now doing a roaring trade. Some smart and ambitious people, quite a few brave women folk among them, had seen the need for goods at the goldfields and thought they probably had a better chance of striking it rich by selling wares to the miners rather than trying to find the gold themselves. Alcohol was one of the many wares that the miners consumed in large quantities. Stores and hotels were popping up all over the goldfields.

"I am beginning to think that my claim is worthless," said Robert to his friend as he lifted the glass and took a large swig of rum. He felt the strong liquor burn all the way to his stomach.

After many rounds of drinks they left the hotel, somewhat the worse for wear, and staggered out onto the street. Not far from their camp, they came across a boxing match that some industrious person had instigated to entertain the miners. Despite his slightly inebriated state, Robert decided it would be a good idea to enter the boxing match. There was, after all, a small purse to be won and his funds were running short. If he didn't find gold soon he would be forced to head back to the farm with his tail between his legs.

As he waited for his turn in the makeshift ring he sobered up somewhat. But not enough to come to his senses and decide against the fight. At last, it was his turn. As he entered the ring, he sized up his opponent; another digger who was not quite as tall as Robert and probably a bit older. Robert thought he had a good chance of winning the bout. The bare fisted fight began. The two men met in the middle and started moving warily around each other. They both threw a couple of punches, which did not find their mark. But then Robert's opponent landed a punch on Robert's chin. Robert staggered and fell to the ground. His anger stirred as his friend helped him up. Robert moved around his opponent again. His anger did nothing to help him though. He threw another loose punch, which barely touched his opponent's jaw as the man ducked quickly. And just as quickly, his opponent threw another punch, which landed squarely on Robert's jaw. This time, Robert was down for the count. When his friend came to his aid to drag him out of the fight, he went willingly. He knew when he was beaten.

Despite his run of bad luck, Robert was determined that he would not go back to his family empty-handed. He knew that his mother had not thought his coming to the goldfields a good idea and, of course, the self-righteous Charles had scoffed at him. Robert's defeat in the boxing ring caused him to re-assess. He decided it was time for him to take this venture more seriously. He was here to find gold, not to win boxing matches. From now on, he would keep his head down. He even curtailed his late-night drinking.

Robert's altered lifestyle quickly reaped rewards and it was not long before he saw that much longed for glimmer in his pan. He couldn't quite believe his eyes as he excitedly washed off the remaining sand and was left with gold! At last, something to show for his efforts.

He stowed away the small amount of gold and dug up another shovel full of sand from the same area. The next pan also showed gold as he washed the sand away. This time, the nuggets were larger. He worked on and by the end of the day, he knew that his claim was not worthless.

He wandered over to his friend's claim.

"Ah, there you are. Would you believe it? I have finally had some luck! What about you?" Robert said to his neighbour.

"Yes, I have had a good day too."

The two headed off to find the gold buyer to discover what their findings were worth. Robert was delighted to find that his gold weighed in at just under one ounce and the gold buyer handed over nearly £9. Not a bad day's work. The next stop was the hotel, to celebrate their good fortune. That night, they both consumed more than a little rum.

Robert worked his claim for the next few weeks, and his luck was in. He amassed a substantial amount of gold, 16 ounces in all and cashed that in for the tidy sum of £150. He felt like a rich man, considering his last wool payment had been £15. Most people could only hope to earn about £20 for an entire year of working. Weighing up his good fortune, he decided it was time to return to the farm. He had already been away longer than he had intended.

ele

1851 Hanging Rock

Harriet stood by the fire in their small but comfortable cottage. She had a hearty stew bubbling away in the pot. Albert had killed a sheep and the vegetable garden was producing well and, of course, they had potatoes. They would eat well tonight.

She took a break from cooking and went outside to her seat under the verandah. The eucalypts were sprouting fresh growth and under their tall canopy the wattles bloomed bright yellow, bringing the promise of warmer weather. The paddocks were green with lush spring growth. Harriet looked over at her garden, thinking that she really needed to spend some time pulling the weeds that were growing so quickly in the early spring sun. It was hard to keep up with all the chores on the farm, as well as her garden. But her garden was her primary joy and she liked the neat rows to be weed free.

Harriet heard the clatter of horses' hooves and looked up to see a rider approaching at a frantic pace on a fine-looking horse. As he drew closer, she realised it was Robert. A smile lit up her face. She had missed him terribly whilst he had been away. She ran to meet him, closely followed by Rebecca.

The others had seen him approaching too. Albert, Charles and George arrived from the front paddock where they had been drafting sheep, and Susannah appeared from the cottage next door to Albert and Harriet's.

Robert charged up to the front of the cottages, waving his hat over his head in greeting.

"I did it!" He shouted, "I found gold!"

The family looked at each other in amazement. Had he really struck it rich?

That evening, the whole family gathered around the rough wooden table in Albert and Harriet's cottage. They listened intently as Robert told them that despite thinking he would never strike gold, he had eventually succeeded.

"Not only did I find enough gold to buy that majestic horse but..." he paused, making them wait to hear the most exciting news.

"We have enough, not to make us rich, but definitely to purchase more stock and some of the other things that we really need. I will be able to start my horse breeding program. I plan to import some well-bred bloodstock from England."

"So, Mother, I told you I would be back. There is probably still plenty of gold for the taking, but now that I have enough to do what I want, they can keep that gruelling work."

"Well congratulations, son," said Albert. Harriet could tell that Albert was proud of what Robert had achieved. Robert had always tried so hard to impress his father and he had achieved something they could only have hoped for. As a close family, Harriet knew they would all benefit from this good fortune. They shared the wonderful meal that she had prepared and drank a toast.

Charles was also delighted at the wonderful news and congratulated his brother heartily. He was immediately thinking about what this might mean for his own plans.

Charles was working hard. He desperately wanted to try his luck in Melbourne. The sheep had been producing good quality fleece and there was an enormous market for wool in England, so he had already made some headway towards his goal of moving to Melbourne and starting his business. He was an accomplished wheelwright and was sure that he could build a profitable business in the city if only he could just amass a nest egg to begin with. The discovery of gold made him think. But in a totally different direction from where Robert's mind had gone. Already there was a tremendous need for carters to take supplies to the goldfields.

Shortly after Robert returned to the farm, Charles decided it was time to implement his plan. Melbourne fascinated him. Port Phillip had become a separate colony in July 1851, with the new name of Victoria. Melbourne had been declared the capital and had become the centre of the colony's wool exporting trade. This, together with the gold rush, meant that the city was booming.

Charles was very keen to convince his brother that he should help to finance a business in the city. It was late afternoon, and the men had been working hard all day harvesting potatoes. They sat under the verandah at Robert's cottage, enjoying a companionable drink and watching the sun setting behind the gums. It was a pleasant sight, with the last of the daylight filtering through the trees.

Charles felt the time was right to speak to Robert about his plans.

"Robert, I am very pleased that you made some gains at the goldfields. But I am essentially a man of business. We have a good life here on the farm, but I also think I could do well with my wheelwright trade if I go to Melbourne. What do you think? And perhaps we could also start a carting business to supply the goldfields. I hear people are making a lot more money supplying goods than the miners are actually making trying to get the gold out of the ground."

"I think you are right, Charles. A business venture is what we need to add to our farming capital."

"Would you be willing to help finance the venture? We could go into business together."

"I think it's certainly worth considering. But I will need some time to think about it. You know how important my horse breeding is to me. I am not sure I want to change direction now. I don't want my plans to suffer because I go into business with you."

"All right, I understand Robert," agreed his brother. "But please don't take too long deciding. If we are going to do this, we need to get started in order to take advantage of the gold rush and the prosperous times in Melbourne."

Robert took longer than the impatient Charles would have liked, but eventually he agreed to provide some finances to establish the new business. Charles was elated and immediately started preparing for his move to Melbourne. With capital from Robert and the money he had already saved, he would have plenty to set himself up in business.

Once he had Robert convinced, he also spoke to his mother and father. None of the family ever made big decisions without consulting them.

"Mother, I believe I should try my luck in the city. I think there are lots of opportunities to be had. Robert has agreed to help with finance. And we think we can cash in on the gold rush by setting up a carting business." Harriet did not object to the plan, giving her oldest son her blessing.

"Well Charles, I think you should follow your instincts," she sighed. "But I will miss you."

His father sat quietly, listening to Charles explain his plans to his mother.

"I agree with your mother, Charles. You have always been the ambitious one of the family and I think you can do well in the city. Just don't forget that your mother will want to hear from you often and you have the farm here that will require some of your attention. We will expect you to return often."

So, with the blessing of his family, Charles set off for Melbourne to seek his new fortune.

Chapter Six

1852 Melbourne

The road to Melbourne had not improved much, but Charles's horse was strong. He took only the few essential supplies that he would initially need, the rest he could purchase in Melbourne as he acquainted himself with the town and what it had to offer. He made it to the outskirts in a few short days.

First, he did some exploring. As he suspected, the city had grown substantially in the months since he first arrived in Port Phillip. But the gold rush meant that many had downed tools in the city and headed for the goldfields. The city was crowded, but mostly with immigrants passing through to the diggings after having made the long voyage from far-off lands in order to seek their fortune. A huge tent city had grown up on the banks of the Yarra River. People were simply pausing to stock up with everything they needed before heading for the diggings. Charles felt his instincts would prove correct. The goldfields would need supplies that would have to come from the city. There would be plenty of opportunities for a man of his skills.

He leased a property in the city's west and set up his business. It didn't take long before he became renowned for his skills as a wheelwright and his business took off. Soon, he was able to purchase his first Melbourne property. But it wasn't enough for the ambitious Charles. He wanted to take greater advantage of the gold rush. Once he established himself, he took a trip back to the farm to try to convince Robert of the benefits of investing more into the city business. He needed to visit his mother and father anyway, as he had so far not kept his promise to return regularly. After catching up with them, he checked on his farm. The sheep were doing well and the potato crop he had planted before leaving was ready to harvest. Next, he went looking for Robert.

"Thank you for looking after the farm, Robert," he said. "We will soon need to employ more shepherds as the flock is growing so rapidly. And I wanted to speak to you again about a carting business. If we go ahead with this idea, we will both need to spend a bit more time in the city until we get established."

Robert frowned. Whilst he loved his life on the farm, the extra work they had all had to take on now that Charles was mostly in Melbourne had been hard on them all.

"It has been tough, Charles. I am not sure that it is a good idea to expand the Melbourne business. At least not until we can get some more help. I have the new horses to consider as well. Come, let me show them to you. They are true thoroughbreds."

Charles was indeed impressed at the magnificent horse-flesh his brother presented to him, a fine-looking mare and stallion directly imported from Britain. Robert reached into his pocket and held out his upturned hand to each horse. They greedily munched the pieces of carrot that Robert proffered.

"They cost a pretty penny, of course, but once we get the breeding program going, it will all pay off," said Robert.

"I understand Robert; they are fine looking animals and I know you will do well with your breeding program. But now that the Melbourne business is established and doing well, I believe it is time to purchase a dray and a team of bullocks so that we can begin carting."

Robert was not immediately convinced. He had discovered that carting was a risky business.

"Charles, I know that you have your heart set on this, but there are risks, you know. The newspapers are full of accounts of how bad the roads are between Melbourne and the gold-fields. There has even been a petition raised and sent to the government. But to no avail, the roads are still terrible and, of course, they are being made worse by all the traffic. That corduroy road through the Black Forest is treacherous after rain. I have heard many a grisly tale from people passing through, of bullocks dying horrible deaths because they couldn't be released from the sucking mud."

"Robert, I am aware of the risks, but I think the rewards will be worth it. If we are careful and make sure that we don't cart in the dead of winter, we will be alright."

Robert was hesitant, but once again, he agreed to provide finance and join his brother in the city for a short time to help him set up the carting business. They purchased six bullocks and a large flat dray and then started the search for suppliers. This proved to be more difficult than they had anticipated. Men were walking off the job to try their luck on the goldfields and so manufacturers and food suppliers were struggling to keep workers. But Charles would not let this stop him. The brothers paid premium prices for the goods but were soon doing regular trips between Melbourne and the diggings in Mt Alexander, Ballarat and Bendigo. They were careful with their animals and only carted when conditions were favourable, having learned from the experiences of others. There was no carting done once the wet weather set in. The business was lucrative, as they could charge £100 per ton for carting goods from Melbourne to Bendigo.

They carted all types of goods. People needed canvas for shelter, shovels and picks needed to be replaced, not to mention feeding the diggers, providing mutton, flour, tea, salt, and sugar. And, of course, there were the sly grog shops and hotels that were springing up everywhere and they needed to be supplied, although many of them had illicit stills and distilled their own potent beverages.

And so, the business in Melbourne grew. But Robert's heart was still in the country. He loved his horses. So, whilst Charles spent most of his time in the city, Robert preferred to get back to the farm as often as possible.

This turned out to be a perfect arrangement. As luck would have it, their interests and skills led them to invest in two of the most profitable trades of the growing nation and they reaped the benefits of sheep farming and carting goods to the goldfields for some time.

Robert met his match in the strikingly beautiful Charlotte. She was slightly taller than him, with blond hair and blue eyes. Like him, she was feisty and quick-tempered. But unlike Robert, her temper cooled easily and she was quick to make amends for any slight she caused.

Robert met her on one of his business trips to Melbourne. Charles was already developing contacts in the right places. On this particular evening, they were both invited to a grand dinner party at the home of one of Melbourne's wealthy businessmen. The stately double storey home in Collins Street was furnished with high-quality fittings and elaborate décor. Many servants moved in and around the guests, seeing to their every need. The brothers were feeling very smug about having received this invitation.

They had not been there long before Robert saw Charlotte across the room. She was serving the guests with delightful canapes on a large silver tray. Even in the plain black dress, crisp white apron and bonnet worn by all the servants, her beauty was clear.

"Who is that woman over there?" Robert asked his brother.

Charles gave his brother a sideways look. "I don't know Robert. Just some servant girl. Why?"

"She is quite beautiful, isn't she?" replied Robert.

"Well, yes, she is quite beautiful, but I don't like that look in your eye, Robert. We are attempting to build our reputation in this city. It would not do for you to fraternise with a servant girl, no matter how lovely."

Robert ignored his brother's concerns and sidled quietly up to the young servant and introduced himself.

"Hello," he said. "My name is Robert Blayney. It is a pleasure to make your acquaintance."

"I am sorry, sir," said the startled young woman, "I really must not converse with the guests. My master is watching over there."

Robert knew that a woman with few prospects would consider that she was fortunate to have found work in this fine home of a wealthy landholder. Of course, he did not want to do anything to jeopardise her chances of keeping the position.

"Never mind him. He is a good friend of mine. I can make excuses," whispered Robert, turning side on, so that their conversation was less obvious. "I am sure he would expect you to be polite to the guests, at the very least."

"Please sir, I really must continue with my work."

"Very well. If you agree to meet me on your day off, I will leave you alone."

Robert felt sure that the young lady was curious, despite her concerns.

"Very well, sir. I have some time off on Saturday. I will try to meet you in the Carlton Gardens after lunch." She hurried off to the kitchen to replenish her tray.

Robert was very pleased with himself and went off to rejoin Charles, who was making the most of this opportunity to greet all the local businessmen.

"Well?" asked Charles, feeling anxious that Robert was going to destroy all his good work of building a reputation as a gentleman of means.

"She has agreed to meet me on her day off."

Charles sighed. He knew there was little point in trying to divert his brother from this course.

Saturday dawned crisp and clear. It was a lovely day for a rendezvous in the gardens. Robert dressed carefully in dark striped trousers and a long, fitted jacket topped off with his favourite bowler hat, and he carried his ornately carved cane. Despite his usual bluster and his blase attitude when discussing the meeting with Charles, he was actually feeling rather nervous about meeting the lovely young lady again. He had had little experience with ladies except for his own mother and sister.

He wandered into the gardens after lunch and walked around for a time, admiring the well-tended lawns and garden beds. Spring was in the air and the garden beds were full of colourful petunias and pansies all just coming into bloom. Robert grew impatient as he waited and started to doubt that she would come. But finally, he spotted her walking towards him.

"Hello," she said, somewhat shyly. To Robert's untrained eye, she looked stunning in the spring sunshine. She was dressed in a dark blue outfit with the bodice tightly laced over her tiny waist. The skirt was full and swept the ground. She wore a pendant over the high neckline of her bodice. Her hair was tightly curled at the front and drawn back into a bun at the rear. Perched on top of her head was a pretty bonnet decorated with a brightly coloured array of feathers and tied under her chin with a bow. She carried a white parasol, trimmed with lace, to keep the harsh colonial sun from her fair complexion.

As she got closer to him, Robert caught a whiff of her delicate eau de cologne. He was mesmerised.

"Hello," he replied. "I am so glad you came. I was beginning to wonder if you would stand me up."

"Well, I am a little concerned. It is rare that I am approached by such a man as you, sir," she replied candidly.

"Let me introduce myself properly. We only spoke in haste when we first met. I am Robert Blayney, landholder and businessman. My brother Charles is an important man in the city and we are building our business together. I also own a farm near Hanging Rock and am a horse breeder."

Robert felt that she seemed a little taken aback by the forthrightness of this statement. He needed to refrain a little from trying to impress her.

"What is your name?" he asked gently.

"My name is Charlotte Kinsley."

Charlotte appeared to become more at ease as they continued to stroll around the gardens. They chatted casually, and Robert told her more about himself and his family. As she relaxed, Charlotte told Robert about her journey to Port Phillip. She had travelled to the colony on her own, aboard the James T. Foord in 1849, when she was just 23. Charlotte explained that she had known that she had few prospects in England and so had come to Port Phillip to improve her life. She admitted she had indeed been incredibly lucky to have secured a post in such a fine household. The pair spent an enjoyable afternoon together, strolling in the gardens, and agreed to meet again the following Saturday.

The meetings became a habit. Charlotte soon had Robert under her spell, he was entranced. But he was also somewhat concerned. He had not revealed to her the secret that he worked so hard to conceal, that he had arrived as a convict. As his feelings for her grew deeper, he knew that he would have to ask her to meet his family eventually. He wanted to ask for her hand in marriage. He wondered if his family would keep his secret.

Robert decided introducing Charlotte to his brother Charles would be a good place to start, so on one of their visits to the gardens, he broached the subject with her.

"Charlotte, I would really like you to meet my brother," he said, looking at her from the corner of his eye.

"Oh, really Robert. I am not sure I am ready to meet your family. Charles sounds awfully important."

"Well, yes, he has made a name for himself in the city, but actually, despite being a bit pompous, he is really quite agreeable."

"Perhaps we could have tea at Russell's Tea Rooms next Saturday," he suggested.

"Very well. I suppose it would do no harm to make his acquaintance. And I have longed to visit those tea rooms."

After he had left Charlotte, Robert went to break his important news to Charles. He entered his brother's book lined study rather sheepishly. Robert was not a reader and he wondered how many of these books, which Charles had collected in his short time in Melbourne, had actually been read by his brother.

"Charles, do you have a moment?" said Robert, still quite loathe to broach the subject.

"Of course, dear brother. What is on your mind?"

"Well, I have met someone," said Robert.

"About time," said Charles.

"You can talk. You are still a lonely old bachelor, too. Intent on making your fortune, you pay no attention to the fairer sex. Well, I have met an amazing woman and I have invited her to have tea with us next Saturday so you can meet her."

"Oh, very well. I suppose I can spare the time."

"But there is something I need to tell you first."

"And what, pray tell, is that?"

"Well... she is the servant I met at that function we attended."

"What? Surely you are not serious, Robert. Here we are trying to establish ourselves as important gentlemen in this town and you want to court a servant girl."

"I understand your concern, but wait until you meet her. She has not always been a servant. When her parents died, she was left without means but she has had an education of sorts when she was young. She is well mannered and delightful. She could easily be mistaken for a high-class lady." As he made his point with Charles, Robert was inwardly cringing. He felt sure that Charlotte would be disappointed that he felt the need to sell her merits to his brother in this manner.

"Very well. I suppose I will not be able to discourage you, so I will at least meet her."

Robert and Charles were waiting patiently in the tea rooms the following Saturday when Charlotte arrived looking charming and well dressed, as usual.

They spent a delightful afternoon together. The menu included scones with cream and jam and delicate iced cakes. Soon the three of them were chatting freely, with Charlotte easily joining in the conversation. It was obvious that she could hold her own in any discussion.

When it was time for Charlotte to leave, Robert accompanied her the short distance to her master's home. When he returned home, he found Charles sitting in his study with a glass of wine.

"Well, what do you think?" asked Robert anxiously as he poured a glass for himself from the crystal decanter.

"She is a servant, Robert," said Charles.

"Yes, but you must admit, she is charming and intelligent, Charles, and quite exquisite. Don't you think she would fit into our circle?"

"Well, yes, I actually suspect you are correct, Robert. She can certainly hold her own in a conversation with gentlemen," he agreed quietly, although the look of slight concern did not leave his face.

"So, what are your plans, Robert?" he asked.

"Well, to be honest, I intend to ask her to marry me," said Robert.

"Oh really? You are that serious? I suppose you won't be talked out of it?" said Charles. Robert frowned until Charles continued.

"Well, dear brother, despite my reservations, I am happy for you. Charlotte does seem to be a sensible woman and I am sure she will be good for you. And if it means you spend more time in the city, then that is also a good thing."

Now that he had introduced Charlotte to Charles, Robert could not put off the inevitable any longer. He must arrange for Charlotte to meet his parents. His father was unwell and Charles was going back to the farm to try to convince him to travel to Melbourne to consult a doctor so that trip presented a good opportunity.

1852 Hanging Rock

"Charles, what are we to do? Your father is so unwell and in dreadful pain." Harriet sat by the fire in Charles' cottage sipping the cup of tea he had made for her.

Charles knew how hard his father had worked since he arrived here at Hanging Rock. Albert had already endured so much trying to eke out a living in Beguildy. Although they were doing well on land that they could now call their own, it was a harsh environment and the work of setting up and running the farms was punishing and relentless.

"I know mother, I have seen him trying to work. He needs to slow down. We have plenty of hired help now to do the farm work. But I agree, we definitely need to do something. I think we should try to get him to see a doctor."

"Oh Charles, if only he would. He is so stubborn and seems to think this will pass. But it gets worse each day."

"Let me talk to him mother, I will see if I can convince him."

That evening, Charles called into his parents' home. Rebecca opened the door with a concerned look.

"I really hope you can talk father into seeing a doctor," she said. "It is awful seeing him in such pain all the time."

"I can only try Rebecca," replied Charles.

"Hello Father," said Charles, entering the warm cosy room. The family could afford some creature comforts now that the city business and the farms were doing so well. Albert sat in an easy chair by the open fire with a rug covering his legs.

"Father, I need to talk to you. You are not well."

"I am fine, son."

"No, you are not Father. I see you struggling to move around. You need to see a doctor."

"Right, and how do you propose I do that? Doctors are not thick on the ground in these parts."

"I know, and that is why I think you should take a trip to Melbourne to see someone. There might be some treatment that they can prescribe. Wouldn't you prefer to get rid of this pain?"

Albert looked at him and then looked away. Harriet took her turn to try to convince him.

"Albert, I hate seeing you like this. Please consider what Charles is saying. You really must see a doctor."

Albert looked at his wife. He could not deny her anything.

"Alright then," he conceded. "I will go, but I doubt it will amount to anything. I am sure there is not much these smart city doctors will be able to do."

Charles arranged for a coach to transport his parents to Melbourne. It would be an exhausting journey for his father, made more so by the pain that would be caused by the jolting over the rough tracks. Finally, though, Albert was able to see a doctor. The doctor examined his hands, which had grown crooked and swollen. He asked Albert if his other joints were painful.

"Yes, I have pain all over," replied Albert.

"Well, I think you have rheumatism. There is very little that I can prescribe."

"But there must be something you can do?" said Harriet, wringing her hands.

"We could try splinting your joints, but I think the best course of action is simple bed rest. I will also give you Laudanum for the pain. Some people are getting relief using eucalyptus oil. Joseph Bosisto is making quite a name for himself, producing this oil to be rubbed on the joints. You could probably try that as well."

Albert and Harriet thanked the doctor and promised to try these remedies. Harriet was thankful for the Laudanum, which she hoped would reduce Albert's pain.

1852 Melbourne

"Hello Charlotte, it is lovely to meet you," said Harriet. Robert's parents were staying overnight at Charles's Melbourne residence following Albert's appointment with the doctor.

"This is my husband, Albert," said Harriet. Albert merely smiled at the lovely young girl.

"Hello, it is lovely to meet you too," replied Charlotte shyly. Robert had told her that his mother would like and approve of her, but he knew that had not eased Charlotte's mind. But he could see that his mother was making every effort to make Charlotte comfortable and she seemed to relax.

They all sat in the elegantly appointed and comfortable sitting room whilst Charles's housekeeper served tea and dainty iced cakes on fine china patterned with tiny roses. Charlotte and Harriet were soon chatting amiably.

Robert turned quietly to his father.

"Well, Father, what do you think?" Robert was desperate for his father's approval.

His father sighed and smiled at his son. "I have only just met her Robert, how can I be expected to form an opinion? But I am sure that if you have chosen her, she will be worthy of your attention."

Robert was extremely pleased that the meeting with his parents had gone so well. Buoyed by this success, he decided it was time to ask for Charlotte's hand. He nervously organised a special evening where they enjoyed a delicious meal complete with fine wine.

"What do you think of this wine, Charlotte?" Robert asked.

"I am enjoying it very much," she replied.

Robert knew he needed to stop making small talk. He had to summon up the courage to ask the question that was at the front of his mind. He rose and took Charlotte's hand and pulled her to her feet.

"Charlotte, will you marry me?" he asked.

Charlotte blushed, but a brilliant smile lit up her face.

"Yes, Robert, I will."

Robert felt his heart swell. He couldn't quite believe that she had agreed to his proposal. But as he watched his beautiful bride-to-be, he noticed the smile slip from her lips.

"What is it, Charlotte?" he asked

"I am just feeling a little melancholy," she replied.

"Why Charlotte, you seemed so happy with my proposal just a moment ago."

"Oh Robert, I am. Please forgive me. I am just thinking of my family back in England. I am here on my own and will have no family to attend my wedding. Who will escort me down the aisle? Who will stand up for me?"

"Oh, my darling, now it is my turn to be sorry. In my great joy at you accepting my proposal, it did not occur to me that you have no family in Australia. Is there not someone that you know who could be your attendant?"

"Well, I suppose I could ask my friend Louisa. She is one of the other servants. She has been very good and kind to me. But I believe I will walk down the aisle on my own."

Neither of them wanted a long engagement, so preparations for the wedding began immediately.

"Robert, what am I to wear?" Charlotte asked him as they discussed their plans whilst strolling around the gardens on their usual Saturday afternoon outing.

"Charlotte, my darling, you must allow me to pay for a wedding dress for you. It would not do for a man of my standing in the community not to provide for his wife-to-be." He gave her a sheepish smile, knowing that his pompous speech would not impress her. However, she agreed to allow him to purchase her gown.

The wedding took place on October 9, 1852. The day dawned clear and sunny, with a cool breeze. Robert, resplendently dressed in his black wedding suit with waistcoat, turned-up collar and bow tie, waited nervously at the altar of the ornate St. James Anglican Cathedral. It was a stunning setting with a dark timber ceiling and fittings and a beautiful stained-glass window framed by a large archway over the sanctuary.

Robert's breath caught as Charlotte appeared. He beamed at his wife-to-be as she walked down the aisle. Charlotte was adorned in a stunning off-white satin wedding gown, with a high neckline and lacey bodice. The sleeves were puffed and met long white gloves at the elbows. The dress emphasised her tiny waist, and the skirt was gathered with yards of the creamy material falling softly to the floor, the train spread out behind the dress. She wore a soft flowing veil that touched the floor with flowers adorning the headband and a matching floral bouquet.

All Robert's family attended the wedding. Albert and Harriet had managed to make the trip to Melbourne, even though Albert was still in very poor health and the long trip had been exhausting for him. They had all arrived a few days prior to the wedding and Rebecca had thoroughly enjoyed spending some time seeing the city. George and Susannah took advantage of the visit to look at houses as they were hoping to buy a city residence so that George could return to his tailoring trade.

After the wedding, they all retired to Charles's home. Charles and Robert had provided a sumptuous wedding feast. They had invited a range of important guests, so they were keen to impress. The crystal wine glasses, silver cutlery and fine china glistened on the long table set for the feast. Guests helped themselves to an amazing array of cold pheasant, poached meats served with aspic, oysters and ices, custards and tarts. The wedding cake stood as the centrepiece of the table, lavishly decorated with pink frosting, ribbon and surrounded by carefully crafted fondant roses.

The party continued late into the night as the wine continued to flow. Robert and Charlotte escaped shortly before midnight and made their way to a hotel in the city where they would spend their wedding night.

1852 Hanging Rock

Once all the formalities of the wedding were complete, Robert was eager to get back to the farm. He had been away for a long time and he missed his horses. On a bright spring morning, they boarded the Cobb & Co coach. The journey between Melbourne and the farms was becoming easier in the well-fitted coach pulled by a team of four horses. Their luggage was tied securely on top. They stopped at an inn for the first change of horses and were able to get some refreshments whilst they waited. They spent the night at another inn along the way and arrived at Woodend the following day. George was there to meet them.

"Hello," he called cheerfully as the two brothers shook hands. The horse stood patiently, swishing his tail as George helped Robert load their luggage into his cart.

"It's lovely to see you again, Charlotte," said George.

"And you too, George," she replied. "I am quite excited to see Robert's farm. He has told me so much about it and all the work you have all done in such a short time."

They all climbed into the cart and George took up the reins and the patient horse moved off at a gentle pace.

The next day, Robert showed Charlotte around the farms. They wandered around amongst the animals and the garden that his mother and Rebecca tended so carefully.

"You have done very well for yourself, Robert," she said, stroking the nose of one of his horses.

"Thank you, Charlotte. I was hoping you would like my farm. I know you are more of a city girl. But I love it here with my horses. I really hope you will be happy as well."

"Well, it is a lifestyle I think I can get used to," she replied. "It is very different, but I am sure we can make our home here comfortable and I will get used to working on the farm with you. Your mother's garden is going well. Perhaps I can learn how to grow vegetables."

Soon the couple settled into the day to day running of the farm. Whilst Robert preferred to spend most of his time on the farm, he and Charlotte travelled back to Melbourne frequently to help Charles in the city business.

Chapter Seven

1852 Melbourne

C harles stared in amazement. Michael had just arrived unannounced at his place of business. Charles could not believe his eyes. Here was the brother whom he had not seen for 8 years standing in front of him. He could tell that the convict sentence had taken its toll. Michael looked a lot older, and he was much thinner. His face was ravaged and one eye was covered with a black eye patch. The patch did not, however, cover the jagged scar that showed beneath his eye. Had his brother lost an eye? The one eye that Charles could see had a haunted look. It was obvious that Michael had been working hard, however, as his physique was much stronger looking than Charles remembered. Before leaving Wales, Michael had not been the hardest worker of the family.

"How did you find me?" Charles asked.

"Well, that is a fine way to greet your long-lost brother," said Michael.

"Oh, I am sorry. It is just such a surprise. How are you?"

"Well, I am alive," replied Michael. "I made it through and have come out the other side. I am not sure if I will ever be able to forget the iron chains, and the cruelty of the guards. But I am glad to be free after all this time."

"But really, how did you find out that I was in Melbourne?"

"It was pure chance. After I received my pardon, I decided to come to Victoria. After all, I was not allowed to return to Wales, but I definitely wasn't going to stay in that hellhole of Van Diemen's Land. I hadn't been here long and was sitting minding my own business in the Old Governor Hotel, having a glass of ale, when I overheard someone mention the name of Blayney. I didn't imagine there would be many people around these parts with that name, so I wondered if it was Robert they were talking about. I know he never made it to Van Diemen's Land, so I thought maybe he was here. In any case, I approached the man and he told me all about you."

As Michael was explaining all this, Charles's mind had been whirling. He had so many questions. He did not know how his brother had fared, having spent so long in Van Diemen's Land. Would he be a broken man? Or perhaps he had become a hardened criminal. Had he stayed out of trouble whilst serving his time? But this would all have to wait.

"What about the rest of the family?" asked Michael.

"They are all here," exclaimed Charles. "We all immigrated in 1850 and have land at Hanging Rock in the interior. We must go and see the family." He was not at all sure where to start with his brother.

"How is Mother?" asked Michael. All the boys had a soft spot for their mother. Even the toughest of them.

"She is well enough. We are all glad that she convinced us to come to Port Phillip. But our father's health is failing. He has rheumatism and is in a lot of pain. He seems to get worse every day and cannot do much at all now."

"Where are you staying?" Charles asked. "You must come and stay with me, of course, until we can get ready to travel to Hanging Rock."

Charles went with Michael to his lodgings where they gathered his meagre belongings.

Within a few days, Charles had made preparations for their trip to Hanging Rock. He and Michael climbed into the buggy and they were on their way. As they started out, Charles asked Michael what it had been like in Van Diemen's Land.

"Well, it was no picnic, that is for sure. I tried to keep my nose clean and mostly I managed." Michael fell silent, and Charles was not at all sure how far to push his brother to tell him more, but as the long journey to Hanging Rock continued, Michael told his story.

"As you know, I got 10 years. I was only a few months in prison in England before they loaded me onto the convict ship, Equestrian, with 300 other unfortunate souls. The voyage was hellish. I have no wish to remember that. And things did not improve once I landed in Van Diemen's Land. We disembarked in Hobart and I was first sent to the Probation Station at Port Cygnet. I was there for fifteen months. We worked on a gang, clearing and cultivating the land and sawing timber. The guards were a tough lot, but overall, I managed to keep my nose clean and last out my probation. Then they sent me to work for a landholder in Richmond. He was not a particularly genial man, and he wielded his whip freely. I was granted a ticket of leave after serving five years. Freedom was sweet, and I tried to get some work in Hobart. I didn't have much luck except for a few odd jobs here and there. I had nothing, no food, so I stole some. But I got caught. I wasn't going to do any more time just for a loaf of bread. Surely they didn't expect me to starve to death. So I took off. But the law caught up with me within a couple of days and although I put up a fight, they threw me in the lockup again. I was charged with larceny and resisting a constable in the execution of his duty. I thought I was done for and heading back to the chain gang. But for some reason my luck changed and I only got a fine. I got some work, paid the fine and stayed out of trouble. Finally, after seven years, I got a conditional pardon, which meant I could leave Van Diemen's Land and travel to Victoria."

Charles had remained silent as Michael told his story. The silence continued for a long time as the cart jolted along the rough tracks. Charles noticed Michael seemed to relax as they left the crowded city behind and ventured into the sparsely populated bush. All around them they could see the signs of last summer's bushfire. Although the gumtrees were all sprouting fresh growth, there were many miles of blackened trunks. As they approached the Black Forest, Michael came out of his reverie.

"And what about you, brother? Tell me what has been happening with you and the rest of the family."

Charles was pleased Michael had broken the silence and went on to describe recent events.

"It has been a trying time in Victoria. We had a close call in the bushfire last year. It burned large sections of the colony out and people lost a lot of animals. The long, hot summer and low rainfall had left the ground tinder dry, and it was such a hot day that the countryside just exploded. We were lucky that the fire passed by us and we had no losses. Then Robert went to the goldfields for a time. He did well. He and I have set up a business in Melbourne."

Michael was sullen as Charles described the brothers' successes, and Charles could not help but feel that Michael was jealous. In an attempt to raise Michael's spirits, he told him a bit about what awaited him at Hanging Rock.

"You know, we all have our own farms. Four choice pieces of land, one for each of us. And we have built four cottages on the farms, so we are all well sheltered. Mother and Father are currently living in one of the cottages, but that will be your farm."

"So you mean to say that I will have to live with our parents?"

"Is that so bad?"

"And what about Rebecca?"

"Yes, she is living there as well."

"Well, that will be cosy, won't it?" said Michael, resuming the awkward silence.

1852 Hanging Rock

Charles had sent word ahead so that when Michael arrived at the farm, Robert and the rest of the family were waiting to welcome him. His mother cried as she embraced him.

"You are so thin," she said.

"Hello Mother. It is good to see you. I am fine, really. It is just good to be finally free of that cursed place."

"But what has happened to your eye?" Harriet wasted no time asking the question that Charles had been wanting to ask ever since Michael had arrived.

"As I told Charles, the man I worked for after my time on the chain gang was not afraid to use his whip."

Harriet's face blanched.

"Oh Michael, that is shocking."

Michael shook hands with his father and spoke in turn to Robert and George. The brothers introduced Michael to their wives.

Robert wondered how well Michael would settle in after his long incarceration. It appeared that his outlook on life had not improved. He knew Michael had always felt badly done by. He suspected they would need to be patient with him as he adjusted to his freedom.

The family shared the fine meal that Harriet had prepared. Robert told them he was considering buying a property in the same street as Charles's new home. Charles caught them up with all the news from Melbourne. He and Robert were doing very well in the business.

Michael was quiet and withdrawn during the meal.

Robert was uneasy. Since arriving at Hanging Rock, he had carefully covered up his past, and no one had yet discovered that he was an ex-convict, and he wanted it to stay that way. He had built a reputation of sorts in this community and didn't want it tarnished. He wondered whether Michael would keep his secret.

After the meal, he found an opportunity to speak to Michael alone.

"What are your plans?" asked Robert

"What do you mean?" replied his brother. "I have only just arrived."

"I mean, do you intend to tell everyone that you have served time?"

"That is really none of your business," said Michael.

"I am an upstanding citizen and a landholder. I have worked hard here to build up the farms and to ensure that our family is respected in this community."

Robert scowled as Michael laughed out loud. He recognised that Michael probably thought he was being pompous.

"And why would that change now?" asked Michael, the contempt in his voice obvious.

"You know why," replied Robert. "You are not known for keeping your mouth shut. You didn't have to involve me in your silly prank that got us both into trouble back in Beguildy."

"And why should you get off scot free when I was going to do time?"

"I would not have been involved at all if you hadn't come up with the idea of shearing those sheep and then selling the wool."

"That's a laugh, Robert. You were just as guilty as me."

Robert felt his temper rising, but he kept it in check. He didn't want to further anger Michael. He could see that he would need to humour him instead.

"Look, all I really want is for you to keep quiet and not tell anyone that we are ex-convicts. You can simply say that you stayed behind in Wales when we all immigrated, but changed your mind when you heard how well we were getting on here."

"Alright, since your respectability is so important to you, I will keep your sad, little secret. But don't cross me, Robert. I have learnt from the best in Van Diemen's Land."

Robert did not feel at all confident, but he just had to hope that Michael would keep quiet.

Unfortunately, Michael did not settle in well. Whilst the rest of the family went about the business of running the farms, he did little to contribute. There was the shearing to be done and the ewes would soon be lambing. But Michael was drinking heavily. He had found his way to the hotel and frequently appeared late for his evening meal, which his mother prepared for him.

Robert was worried. Despite having spoken to Michael, to convince him to help out, nothing had improved. In fact, it was getting worse. Michael was becoming more morose and bad tempered.

One evening, several weeks after Michael had arrived, Charlotte and Robert were sitting under the shade of a large gum just outside their hut, enjoying a cup of tea, when Robert eyed Michael staggering along the track, obviously the worse for imbibing too much rum.

Robert frowned. He was getting quite tired of Michael's attitude, but he really did not feel like an argument tonight. It had been a long, hot day.

Michael staggered over to the couple and sat down.

"Evening, Michael," said Robert.

"Can I get you a cup of tea?" said Charlotte.

"No thank you, Charlotte, though I could use a drop of rum."

"It looks to me like you have had enough," said Robert.

"I don't need you to tell me when I have had enough, thankyou Robert. By the way, I hope you aren't planning to head back to Melbourne for a while. I can't do all the work."

Robert glared at Michael. He was hardly doing all the work. In fact, in Robert's opinion, he wasn't doing anywhere near his share.

"Charles and I are doing very well with our carting business, Michael. With the goldfields still needing a lot of supplies, we will not run out of work anytime soon. I am needed in Melbourne as well as here on the farm."

Michael, however, was not impressed.

"Well, that's wonderful for you both. And meanwhile, I am stuck here trying to run the farm."

It was obvious to Robert that Michael was jealous of the success of his brothers in the city. And now George was also looking to make the move to Melbourne. Robert knew that George did not really enjoy farming life. The brothers still worked their farming properties, but with the exception of Michael, they all had other options. Michael really did not appear to have any ambitions other than to drown his sorrows in alcohol.

Robert could see that Charlotte was more and more uncomfortable with Michael's argumentative attitude which became worse as the conversation went on.

"I must prepare the evening meal now Michael," she said, getting up from her seat. But Michael was angry now, having not had any confirmation that Robert would stay and help out on the farm.

"Oh, don't you go running off. You need to know a few facts about your self-righteous husband." Robert's stomach churned.

"You're drunk Michael," he said. "Go home and sleep it off."

"Oh, drunk am I? Well, at least I can still remember where we both came from. He hasn't told you, has he?" sneered Michael.

"Stop Michael," warned Robert grimly.

"Holier than thou. Likes to pretend he is some big city toff. But actually, he is an ex-con, just like his useless brother."

Charlotte gave Michael a startled look. She turned to Robert, who could not hide the fear in his eyes.

"Go home, Michael," he yelled, raising his fist. Michael, having done his worst, realised it would be best to leave and staggered off to find another tot of rum.

Robert was furious.

"He should not have said anything. He had no right."

Robert could see that Charlotte was overwhelmed by the news, so he managed to bring his anger under control. Gently, he took hold of Charlotte and turned her to face him. He could see the tears welling in her eyes.

"Is it true, Robert? Why didn't you tell me?"

"I am so sorry, my love. I couldn't tell you for fear of losing you. But yes, it is true. Come, sit down and listen to my side of the story."

"Yes, I was a convict and was sentenced to transportation for seven years. It was a hard life where we came from. I am sure you can understand that many people had to do what they could in order to survive. And Michael played a large part. We were both found guilty of shearing sheep that didn't belong to us and then selling the wool. We thought we were less likely to be caught stealing the wool than stealing the sheep. Who would have thought that they would have been able to identify the fleeces?"

He went on to explain his time in Pentonville prison and how he had arrived in Port Phillip with a ticket of leave.

"Oh Robert, you should have told me. It is such a shock."

"Yes, I know Charlotte. Michael should never have told you like that. But you can see that since I have been here that I have made good. I have been a law-abiding citizen and have made my way as a successful farmer and businessman. I want to forget my past. Can you forgive me?"

Charlotte looked at him and he could see the love in her eyes, but also the hurt.

"It is not so much what you have done in the past. I know you are a good man. What upsets me more is that you lied to me."

"Yes, I can see that. But I was worried that I would lose you. Let us promise each other that there will be no more secrets."

They both stood, and Robert held her close.

"I know we can get past this, Charlotte. I love you."

1855 Hesket near Hanging Rock

Life settled into a rhythm for Robert and Charlotte and for the rest of the Blayney family. The Melbourne business went from strength to strength and so too did the farm. But now the word was out that the land around Hanging Rock was fertile and there was good rainfall. The district was fast becoming a great option for new settlers. There was also an abundance of timber which, apart from being a great asset when they built their homes, also provided a source of revenue for the new settlers, as timber was in short supply in the city. Melbourne was growing so rapidly that building materials were at a premium. The Government began surveying the land ready for sale. Areas of land were set aside for towns and so the small communities of Newham and Hesket were born. Not all of this was good for Robert and his family. The population of Victoria had grown to over 77,000 and everyone wanted land. Robert and his brothers had to pay premium prices to keep their farms. It was indeed fortunate that they had done well enough to be able to afford to keep all four farms.

Robert was still worried about Michael. He had not really settled in well to farm life at Hesket. His time in Van Diemen's Land seemed to have really taken its toll. Robert knew that he was jealous that his brothers were all doing well with their city business interests, whilst he languished on the farm. He had also complained to Robert that his mother had too much to say about how he lived. But still Robert was surprised when he saw Michael building another cottage.

"Michael, what is this about? Why are you building another cottage?" asked Robert.

"Well, I need my own space. This farm was meant for me, after all. I am building another place for Mother and Rebecca to live."

Robert was horrified. Their father had died only two years ago. It had been a terrible time and his mother was still mourning the loss of her husband. They had been in the colony for such a short time. Unfortunately, as the doctor had foreseen, the remedies did not halt Albert's disease and within a few months of the diagnosis, he had not been able to not leave his bed. Despite Harriet's constant care and attention, he had passed away in February 1853.

"You can't be serious Michael, surely you would not turn your own mother out of the home she has lived in ever since she arrived here."

"I am sure she and Rebecca will be very comfortable. And besides, I plan to marry one day and need to have my own place."

So, despite Robert's resistance, the building continued.

Robert sought his mother out.

"Mother, I can't believe Michael is being so cruel as to move you out of your home," he said.

"Robert, please don't worry. I will miss my home. But I really don't have the energy to object. I miss your Father so much. I am weary and don't want any more arguments. But I am sure that Rebecca and I will soon become used to a new place. Michael is difficult to live with and maybe if he has his own space and has to look after himself, it might make him appreciate all that Rebecca and I have tried to do for him. So please don't make a fuss."

Rebecca, who had listened to this conversation with a grim look on her face, now weighed in.

"Michael is very cruel and I can't believe he is doing this, either. Frankly, I can't wait to live in our new place without him. He drinks too much and is so argumentative. It will be much more peaceful. He thinks he can get himself a wife. I am really not sure who would have such a mean-spirited man. I pity the woman who takes up with him."

"Now Rebecca, please keep a civil tongue in your head," said her mother. "We know Michael drinks too much, but it is, after all, his decision. We cannot tell him what to do. And remember what he has been through."

Robert felt he had no option but to accept his mother's wishes. So, in due course, Harriet and Rebecca moved out of the main cottage and into the newly erected cottage at the rear. They soon made it comfortable, and Robert began to see the benefits. Michael and Rebecca had far fewer opportunities to bicker with each other, for one thing.

PART TWO

Chapter Eight

1858 Heidelberg

John Marlowe had grown into a fine young man, an inch or two taller than his father, with a handsome face, black hair and a full beard. He stood up to his full height, releasing the sheep he had been shearing and stretching his back. He glanced over to the horizon, where ominous storm clouds were gathering. As he watched, lightning cracked the sky with a brilliant flash followed a second or two later by a gigantic crash of thunder. The wind was picking up and white caps were forming on the churning surface of the Yarra River. This could spell disaster. It had been a temperate spring, and if it turned cold now, the freshly shorn sheep could be in danger. He hoped they would not lose too many. But there wasn't a lot he could do about it. This was all part of farming life.

John had worked hard helping his parents to build up the farm and he revelled in the knowledge that he was contributing to his family's continued good fortune. It seemed a lifetime ago when, in 1844, he and his family - his parents Samuel and Rose and his four siblings - had packed up their belongings in Thornborough, Buckinghamshire and boarded The Abberton barque in Plymouth to start the long journey to Port Phillip. He could still remember the excitement he, as a thirteen-year-old boy, felt at the prospect. He suspected it had been a much more anxious time for his parents, knowing they were leaving everything they knew behind. John was glad his parents had made that courageous decision. He loved it here and marvelled at how the community had grown since they arrived.

Upon their arrival, they had taken up the lease of farming land on the Yarra River at Heidelberg. John remembered the hardships they had endured in their first years in the colony. He often saw a look of despair on his father's face as he tried to make a living in the hot, dry climate. Then there were the devastating floods of 1849. The family had just been starting to get on their feet when the flood waters came barrelling down the Yarra, inundating their land and destroying both crops and livestock. But they had not given up and eventually they had recovered from this ordeal. Now they were reaping the rewards of all their hard work.

John was getting restless now though. He lived with the rest of his family in their small but comfortable cottage. It was sparsely furnished and was no longer really meeting the growing family's needs. His mother had borne three more children since they had arrived. Now the family of ten had to make do with small areas divided by hessian strung from the rafters.

John wondered what else he and his family could accomplish in this great country. He had kept abreast of the growth in the interior and knew that the land was being surveyed and farming lots were up for sale. Like so many other adventurers of the time, he was lured by the promise of wonderful farming land with abundance for all in the outer reaches of the Port Phillip district.

He had been considering this for some months and now he felt it was time to broach the subject with his parents. The couple sat quietly by the fire, Samuel smoking his pipe and Rose working at her needlepoint. John surveyed them both proudly. His father was still strong despite his advancing years and he thought his mother looked well even though she was dressed in the simple attire of a farmer's wife, a brown cotton dress with a high neckline, pin tucked bodice, and full length gathered skirt. He hoped his parents would give consideration to his plan.

"Mother, Father, may I speak to you?" he asked quietly.

"Of course, son, what is it?" replied his father.

"You know I am so proud of what we have achieved since we came to the colony."

"Yes, son, it has turned out rather well, hasn't it? We have everything we need. And you children have even received an education. I doubt all of that would have been possible in England."

"That is true, Father, but I have been considering a new venture. Our family has grown," he said. "I really think it would be good if we moved further into the interior. If we do that, we can actually purchase land rather than just leasing. I have been exploring the land available in Newham."

John saw the shocked look in his mother's eyes.

"Oh, John, do you really think that is wise? We are quite comfortable here. Your Father and I are getting on in age. I really think it would be nice to slow down a bit. I am not sure I like the idea of starting all over again."

"Yes, that is all true, Mother. But we would all have better prospects if we moved to a larger property."

"Where is this place, John?" asked his father. "Are you sure it is good farming land?"

"It is about 60 miles to the Northwest of here. I have heard that many settlers have moved out that way. The talk around town is that the land is fertile and rainfall is generally good. They are advertising new land sales coming up soon in the Government Gazette."

His mother was still looking grim.

"What about the church, John? I have been greatly comforted by being able to keep up some of the traditions of the old country when we came here."

John knew his parents had been especially pleased when they found that there was a Particular Baptist congregation in Melbourne. Samuel and Rose were baptised members of the church and they wanted the same for their children. Apart from leaving home and family in Thornborough, leaving the congregation had been an added sacrifice for them. Meeting up with Pastor Ward had indeed been fortunate and the family became regular worshippers at his services. John enjoyed the services and was glad for his parents that the congregation had welcomed them so readily.

John thought hard. He had not considered how much anxiety it would cause his mother if she could not attend regular services.

"What if I could get Pastor Ward to come to Newham? I am sure there would be other Baptists in a growing community that would also be pleased to attend services."

John went to visit the Pastor and soon had his agreement. He would come to Newham once a month. It meant an opportunity for growing his congregation, after all.

Once this agreement was in place, Rose reluctantly agreed to her son's plans. John felt that although his father had said little during the discussion, he seemed excited at the prospect of further adventure.

John and Samuel began preparations for the move. Fortunately, after years of hard work, they had the means to get together the stock and equipment they needed to venture into the new settlement areas. Soon they had purchased 300 acres of land in the newly established Newham district, in the shadows of Hanging Rock. The family, together with all their belongings, piled into the bullock dray and set off on the long journey from Heidelberg to Newham. It would take several days with the lumbering bullocks. John knew how lucky they were to have acquired these fine animals. They would prove advantageous on their new farm. They were also taking a small number of cattle with which to start off their herd.

1858 Newham

John stared around him in amazement. The family had arrived at their new property in Newham. They had seen so much that was new to them since they had come to Port Phillip. Now that they had left the township, John began to realise just how vast the interior was. The dense bush and areas of open pastoral land seemed endless. They had travelled for miles at a time without encountering another living person. The number of animals they encountered increased. Kangaroos, koalas and possums were just some of the many creatures that appeared in the bush, not to mention the bird life. The family gazed around, in awe of everything they saw, not least were the towering pillars of the outcrop that was Hanging Rock. Their land lay in the shadow of this amazing formation.

John heard his father talking quietly to his mother.

"What do you think, my dear?" Samuel asked his wife. She looked pale and tired. John could see the journey had taken its toll on his delicate mother.

"I don't know what to think, Samuel," she replied. "I had enough trouble adjusting to Heidelberg, but at least here we will have fresh air, I suppose. The town was becoming crowded, and the services were not keeping up. I only hope that we can be happy here."

John was much more enthusiastic than his mother.

"Well, I think it is perfect," he said. "I know it is primitive, Mother. But we will soon have you set up in a wonderful home with all the comforts. You just wait and see."

This was not necessarily an empty claim. John had learned many skills in the short time he had lived in Victoria.

"Yes, John, you are right," said his father with a smile. "We will have everything in shape in no time. Look at the abundance of timber around us."

The family set to work. There was a lot to be done. First, they would need to have shelter. John and his father and younger brothers went about setting up a temporary structure, made from some saplings and canvas they had brought with them. That would keep them sheltered until they could build something more permanent. They set to work on cutting down trees, stripping their bark and sawing them into slats. Slowly, the new home took shape, with the timber slats providing the walls and the bark they stripped from the trees fastened down with logs pegged through it to form the roof. They had brought some furniture and household items with them on the bullock dray. Soon, they had a comfortable home. There was also a significant amount of rock in the area which they used to build sturdy chimneys.

They found that the land was rich, and there was plenty of water from the nearby creek and the springs at Hanging Rock. Their cattle could graze on the land and access the water freely. Before long they had their first planting of potatoes in the ground. They also planted 10 acres of orchard and soon had a range of fruit trees growing.

John was an easygoing young man and was popular with all whom he met. He had worked hard with the rest of the family to set up their new home and he was glad to see the community of Newham was growing, as were the surrounding communities of Hesket and Woodend. It was not long before he and his family were getting to know their neighbours. All the families assisted each other where possible, sharing tools and equipment and working together for the good of the community.

John and his family soon made the acquaintance of Harold Langdon. Pastor Ward had kept to his word and traveled to Newham for monthly services. They often held these services at the Marlowe home, as there was not yet a Baptist church in the region. As the congregation filed in, John noticed the newcomer.

"Welcome to our service," said John, and he introduced himself. "I am John Marlowe, this is my Father Samuel and my mother Rose."

"Thank you," replied the young man. "I am pleased to meet you all. My name is Harold Langdon."

"Are you a Baptist, Harold?" asked John.

"I am not baptised but I am very keen to become a member of this congregation. I have heard a lot about you all, and much of it is very good."

At that moment, the minister rose to begin the service.

Harold sat down next to John.

When the service was over, John and Harold struck up a conversation.

"So, are you a farmer? Do you have property?" John asked.

"Yes, I have a small holding with some sheep and cattle. I also do the mail run to and from Woodend twice a week. I have found this to be good farming land since I arrived. But I have been lonely on my own. I must say, I am very glad to make your acquaintance."

"Yes, it is a lonely life still, although the community is growing quickly. There is a social evening on Saturday night. You should come."

Everyone gathered at the school the next Saturday evening. The community worked hard and was glad of the leisure activity that these social evenings offered. The women took the opportunity to get out of their everyday farm clothes and get dressed up in their Sunday best. Some ladies wore hats whilst others pulled their hair up into elaborate styles tied with ribbons. The men put their dungarees aside and wore waistcoats and jackets. All the men wore either shiny top hats or bowlers. The ladies arrived laden with baskets of scrumptious food for supper, and the band from Woodend played gay tunes for those who wished to dance.

John saw Harold as soon as he arrived and motioned for him to join him and his family.

"Hello Harold," said John, "I am glad you could make it."

"Thank you for inviting me," replied Harold. John noticed that Harold's gaze had settled on his younger sister.

"I would like you to meet my sister, Grace."

Grace smiled brightly at Harold.

"John has told me all about you," she said. "It is good to meet you."

"It is a pleasure to meet you too, Grace," replied Harold.

The three new friends chatted for a while during a break in the music. As the music started up again, Harold asked Grace to dance, and they made their way out onto the dance floor. The three quickly became firm friends.

John worked hard on the family farm and became well known for his willingness to help his neighbours in his new home-town. He was casting his eye around at the young ladies of the district. He was ambitious and had decided that taking a local woman as his wife would give him good standing in the community as a married man. Soon he met Elizabeth. She and her family lived in nearby Woodend after emigrating from England. She was the youngest of five siblings. Her family were members of the Methodist congregation and had contributed to the building of their new church. John met her on social occasions and enjoyed her company. He felt she would be a suitable wife. He spoke to his parents to ask for their advice.

"Elizabeth comes from a good Christian family," his father said. "I believe she would make a very suitable match."

"Yes, I think you are right Samuel," said his mother, as usual, in agreement with her husband.

But before asking for Elizabeth's hand, John wanted to have something to offer her. He purchased a piece of land close to his parents and began building a spacious new home.

Meanwhile, he had continued to court Elizabeth. When the house was ready, he asked her to marry him. She readily agreed.

Elizabeth was delighted that John had built a home for them.

"It is only proper that my new wife should have a home of her own," said John proudly as he showed her around. "It is an honour to welcome you into our new home."

"It is wonderful John, it is much larger than I am used to. I know we will be very happy here." She smiled broadly as she surveyed the cottage and the garden John had planted, including a row of plum trees at the back.

John's ambitions and his popularity among the locals soon saw him becoming the family spokesperson. The growing communities had been dismayed when in 1857, during the first land sales, the Government had been so shortsighted as to sell 170 acres of land which included Hanging Rock into private hands. Only 96 acres to the East of the rock had been retained. The farmers of the district were concerned that their access to the water and grazing around the rock would be curtailed. Hanging Rock was becoming a very popular spot for ramblers and pleasure seekers. Every weekend, people from the surrounding districts and as far afield as Melbourne would visit to climb the rock and enjoy picnics in the bush setting. John was to enter many a battle with those who felt the land should be fenced off for picnic grounds, sports meetings and horse racing rather than allowing the farmers to run livestock on the land.

1859 Hanging Rock

John was busy developing his new piece of land. He was very proud to be able to provide for his wife and looked forward to having a family with her. He looked out over his sheep grazing peacefully in the new paddock he had just finished fencing. As he surveyed his land, he saw Harold Langdon approaching on his horse.

"Have you heard the news, John?" Harold asked as he jumped off his horse.

"What news would that be?" said John, patiently surveying his friend. It had been a long, hot day and he had been working since dawn.

"Apparently, the Hanging Rock land is up for sale again. There is no telling what this will mean as far as access to the land goes. So far, there have been no restrictions, but this could easily change if the land is sold again."

"Come inside out of the sun," said John. "I am sure Elizabeth will make us a cup of tea.

John and Harold took a seat at the kitchen table. It was a simple room dominated by the large timber table and chairs with an open fire at one end, over which hung kettles and pots. Harold could smell something delicious bubbling in a large pot.

"I had heard a whisper that the land was up for sale again," said John when they both had a cup of tea in front of them. "Have you heard who might be interested in buying it?"

"The word is that William Adams and Alexander Archer are both interested. It is a great pity since it is up for sale that the Government doesn't consider buying it back."

"Well, I guess we will need to wait and see what happens," said John. "But I can't help thinking that we need to get more involved, Harold. We need to lobby the Government to buy back the land."

~elle~

The land ended up being sold in two lots. Alexander Archer purchased 100 acres and William Adams purchasing the remaining 72 acres. John suspected that this was not what either man had really wanted. He had heard that William Adams had big plans for the land.

As well as picnics and leisure pursuits at the rock people now also frequented the area for hunting as wildlife was abundant. Hunters shot kangaroos, koalas and all varieties of birds. Rabbits had also been released into the area and provided another target for the shooters. These visitors provided potential for a savvy businessman to take advantage of. But now that William had been thwarted in his attempt to purchase Hanging Rock, it seemed to John that his plans might have to be shelved. This pleased him because he knew that Alexander Archer only wanted to use the land for farming. He had no plans to develop the site which meant that the land could still be used by the entire community, rather than just a select few who wanted to see the area used only for profitable pursuits.

Chapter Nine

1861 Melbourne

C harles sat in the opulent study of his fine house. He was starting to see the fruits of his labour in Melbourne. It had certainly turned out to be a good decision when he and Robert had started the business in the city nearly ten years ago. His carting business was booming thanks to the new rural communities that had grown up between the goldfields and Melbourne, creating a whole new clientele for his goods.

Charles's wife Jane quietly entered the room carrying a tray with tea and cakes.

"Will you stop for tea now, Charles?" she asked.

Charles turned and smiled at his wife. He considered himself lucky that she had agreed to marry him. It was not a particularly romantic relationship, as their marriage was one of convenience. He had needed a wife to adorn his arm at official functions, and she had needed to escape the clutches of a domineering and abusive father. In the 6 years they had been married, they had become firm friends. Jane had a quick mind, which Charles thought was far more suitable than being wed to a simpering woman for romantic reasons only.

He rose from his large oak desk and kissed Jane on the cheek.

"Thank you, my dear," he said as he settled into one of the comfortable chairs close to the open fire. It was cold and dreary outside with scattered showers of rain falling intermittently throughout the day. Charles loved his warm, cosy study, where he spent many hours of his time.

Jane sat down opposite him, poured the tea and handed him the delicate china cup and saucer.

"What are your plans for going to see the family?" she asked.

"Well," said Charles, "they are at it again. Constantly bickering with each other. Robert and Michael are not getting on at all well since Father died."

Jane nodded sympathetically but did not comment. She was growing rather tired of hearing about the family squabbles. But as usual, she wanted to be supportive of her husband.

"Robert tells me that Michael has built another cottage for mother and Rebecca. Robert is none too pleased," said Charles.

"Perhaps it is not such a poor solution." replied Jane. "I think your mother's state of mind has been a bit fragile since your Father died. I am sure she was getting no peace in that household, what with Michael drinking so heavily."

Charles smiled, acknowledging his wife's always sensible opinions about his family.

"In any case, we should pay a visit to Mother."

"Your mother needs your support. It can't be easy for her."

"Of course, there is the official opening of the railway line to Woodend coming up soon. What would you say to attending? They are planning a big banquet for the official opening and then there will be the gala ball afterwards. I think it would be advantageous for us to attend."

"That sounds like quite an adventure," replied Jane. She was always keen to fall in with her husband's plans, especially if it meant being seen in the right circles. She felt sure that other prominent Melbourne citizens would make the most of this opportunity to socialise with some influential people.

"This progress excites me so much," said Charles. "It is wonderful to see Melbourne growing so quickly, and now roads and services out to the surrounding districts are finally catching up."

Charles was still making his way in the big city, working very hard to convince the upper Melbourne classes that he was a gentleman of some standing. Making an appearance on this important occasion would be beneficial to his cause.

1861 Woodend

The grand opening of the Woodend rail line was to occur on July 8, 1861. Charles and Jane dressed in their finest attire, carefully chosen to look impressive but also with a relaxed country feel. They both wore thick overcoats against the cold July day. They left early for the station, their driver whipping up the horse to hurry them along so they would arrive in plenty of time to promenade around the platform and see who else was taking the journey.

As Charles assisted Jane down from the carriage, he spotted another prominent businessman in the crowd. He and Jane hurried over to greet him.

"Are you traveling to Woodend today?" Charles asked his colleague.

"Yes, as a matter of fact, I am and I am quite looking forward to seeing your locality, Charles. It is a splendid day for it," said the businessman. "Rather cold, but at least it is calm and sunny. It is great to see this train line opened."

"Progress, my friend, progress," said Charles, puffing out his chest. He was proud that the train line was going to his home neighbourhood.

Charles looked around and noticed the official party. He knew that the whole of the government ministry, the commissioner of roads, and several prominent businessmen had been invited. He was rather put out that he was not considered important enough to have been included in their number. But it just made him more determined to continue to work to achieve notoriety amongst these men.

Charles and Jane took their seats on the train as the whistle blew in the chilly morning air, announcing the moment of departure. Steam rose and filled the air as the train pulled out of the station and gathered speed.

The train stopped first at Sunbury and the official party left their carriage to admire the newly erected Jackson's Creek Bridge. They stopped at Riddell's Creek station, where more of the official party joined the group. Eventually, after a brief stop at Gisborne station, the train steamed into Woodend. The new station was a fine structure, as befitted the importance of country railway stations. It was built of sawn timber with iron roofing. Wide verandahs over both platforms provided shelter to travellers. The station master stood surveying the scene, proudly waving his flag and blowing his whistle as the first train pulled into his station. He looked around him, keen to ensure the safety of the passengers as they alighted from the train.

After rousing cheers from the small crowd of locals who had come to greet them, the official party made their way to the station goods shed, where a sumptuous lunch, accompanied by a generous amount of champagne, had been laid out for them. Meanwhile, the locals had arranged their own celebration, which Charles and Jane would attend with the rest of their family.

Charles and Jane gathered their luggage and moved off to meet Robert and Charlotte, who were waiting patiently for them under the wide verandah. Robert shook hands with his brother and embraced Jane. Charlotte and Jane embraced warmly. The sisters-in-law had quickly become firm friends. They needed to be allies in this unruly family. The two women chatted happily as Charles and Robert discussed Michael. Charles would have preferred to have this discussion in private, but Robert immediately began to berate Charles about his problems with Michael.

"He is just unbearable," said Robert. "He spends a good deal of his time in the hotel and as for getting any work done..."

"Maybe he needs a woman to help him settle down," replied Charles, trying to keep his voice jovial.

"I am not sure that would help, but who would have him anyway."

"Come Robert, let's leave this discussion for now and enjoy the celebrations."

They stepped down from the station platform and the brothers assisted their wives to climb into the back seat of the cart and then climbed aboard themselves.

Robert flicked the reins and the cart, drawn by two of his finest horses, moved off toward the main street of Woodend, where celebrations would be getting underway for the railway opening. The townspeople were roasting a bullock in the street. It was to be a tremendous occasion. The rest of the family were waiting to meet them there.

As they arrived, Harriet greeted them. She hugged them and said how happy she was to see them. Rebecca stood beside her mother. She, too, embraced both Charles and Jane.

Charles noticed that his mother was thinner and looked rather sad. He knew she missed their father terribly, even after all this time, and he was sure that family bickering was not helping.

"What do you think of your new home, Mother?" asked Charles.

"It is very comfortable, thank you Charles. Rebecca and I are very happy there."

"We are certainly not missing having to live with Michael," retorted Rebecca.

"Now Rebecca, please be civil," said her mother.

"Where is Michael?" asked Charles.

"He should be along soon," replied his mother warily. Charles hoped they could have a peaceful family gathering, but that would not be possible if Michael was in one of his moods. Soon enough, Michael appeared, looking somewhat the worse for wear.

"Well, if it isn't my rich city brother," he exclaimed, the derision obvious in his voice.

"And it is good to see you too," replied Charles.

Charles could see that Michael's attitude distressed his mother. He again appeared to be going to make a scene.

"Let's just enjoy the celebrations," said Charles, trying to keep the peace. "Later, we can have a look around the farms. It has been a while since I visited."

"Yes, it is about time you managed to get back here. We are all keeping the farms running. We could use some more help from you."

Charles ignored that comment. The four brothers had all become wealthy, which meant they had been able to employ shepherds and other labourers to help them run their farms. It was not really an issue that Charles spent a good deal of his time in the city. George and Susannah had by now purchased a home in Melbourne and George was doing well in the tailoring trade. Of course, Robert still spent most of his time in Hesket with his beloved horses.

The celebrations went well into the afternoon with much food and drink being consumed by all present. As the day drew on, the scene began to get rowdy, so Charles suggested it was time that they headed home to inspect the farms. Michael took some convincing, but eventually they were all out overseeing the fruits of their labour over the past 10 years. They admired the sheep grazing quietly in the paddocks and Robert's fine horses. The chickens, turkeys and cows were all valuable assets. They could see the white flowers of a crop of potatoes standing out against the green pastures. They had done well despite their differences.

Charles and Jane stayed on at the farm for another few days. They would be attending the gala ball and banquet that was being planned to celebrate the opening of the railway. It was another opportunity for Charles to build on his reputation as an important landholder and businessman.

Charles looked fondly at his wife as he assisted her down from the jinker. She looked stunning in her silk ball gown with a round neckline and puffed sleeves. It was buttoned down the back with a large bow at the waist. The skirt was decorated with pink silk ruffles. The material of the dress was a shade of pink that had a changeable quality depending on the reflected light.

Charles was delighted with the scene that greeted them as he and Jane entered the impromptu ballroom in the goods shed of the Woodend railway station. Bunting was strung from the ceiling, and colourful banners hung on the walls. Evergreen branches and flowers festooned the entire scene. Hundreds of coloured lamps created magical lighting.

Along one wall was a table of refreshments. The food that the caterer had prepared and brought in from Melbourne was a sumptuous feast. Champagne flowed freely.

The other attendees matched the grandeur of the venue. Many important people from Melbourne had been invited, and they were all dressed in the latest fashion. Ladies wore beautiful gowns decorated with satin flowers and lots of lace. Jewels glistened at their throats and wrists. The men were equally resplendent in their top hats and tails.

1864 Hesket

The problems that the Blayney family experienced with Michael did not diminish over the next few years. Charles hoped he would marry and settle down. However, Agnes, the saucy young girl he had been pursuing, was not the match that any of the family had hoped for.

All the Blayney family were home in Hesket for the holidays. Even George and Susannah had made the trip from Melbourne. Charles was pleased for them. George had never been much of a farmer and seemed much happier now that he and Susannah and their family spent much of their time in the city. He was less pleased, however, that over the last few years, they had tried to remove themselves completely from any family dramas.

As usual, the community had gathered at Hanging Rock and everywhere there were groups of local people enjoying their downtime. Robert and Charles watched on as Michael and Agnes joined in the revelry. They could see Agnes socialising with some other young ladies. Her loud voice and raucous laugh rang out above those of the other girls.

"What do you think of her Charles?" Robert inquired of his older brother. "Surely she is not a fit wife for Michael."

"Well, I am sure I don't know. She is, of course, way too young for him. She is only 15 years old. He is 17 years older than her," replied Charles. "She is his type, I suppose. But from the rumours going around, I am not sure that she won't cause him quite a few headaches. What do you think, George?" he asked his younger brother, who had wandered up at that moment with Susannah.

"Don't ask me. I really don't know anything about her. Nor do I want to," replied George.

Charles sighed. He was becoming accustomed to George's disinterest in the family affairs. He just wished he too could take less of an interest. But Robert seemed to depend on him to help keep some semblance of order in the family.

Charles could not help but notice that the girl that Michael was keen on was a little rough around the edges. But that was probably what actually appealed to Michael, he thought. He was a little rough around the edges himself.

Charles decided he really needed to talk to Michael. He certainly couldn't trust Robert with the task, as that would only start an argument. He sought Michael out and broached the subject.

"You have heard the rumours, haven't you? That she is prone to confrontation and quite happy to take out her problems on whomever gets in her way," said Charles.

"Yes, I am well aware of her shortcomings, thank you Charles," Michael stated indignantly. "But I would rather have a wife with some character and get up and go."

Charles knew this comment was directed at his own wife, Jane. He knew Michael had little time for her and thought her too willing to bow to Charles's wishes.

"But Agnes is only a child, Michael."

"Well, I think I know her better than you and she is far from a child," Michael smiled suggestively.

Charles looked over at Agnes. She was tall and well-built for her tender age. She was not a natural beauty though she had a handsome face, but she had a disturbing way about her and was definitely not afraid to say what she thought.

But it seemed that Michael had made up his mind to marry her. As the wedding day drew near, Charles watched on as the rest of the family whispered about Michael's poor choice.

Rebecca, in particular, did not get on with Agnes and said so.

"Michael, you cannot marry that woman," she said to him, finally summoning up the courage to confront her brother. Since Michael had returned from Van Diemen's Land, she had had several altercations with him.

"Mind your own business, Rebecca," replied Michael curtly. "She can be fiery, but I have no doubt she will make me a good wife and life will certainly not be boring."

"Well, I can definitely agree with that. But what about the fact that she seems to always be in some squabble or other with the neighbours? Hardly the type of person we want to invite into our family."

"Oh, and you can talk!" said Michael. "You have had your fair share of disputes with our neighbours."

Harriet was always trying to quell the tempers of her family and to keep the peace.

"Rebecca, that is enough," she said. "Michael is free to make his own decision about who he marries. Although I do agree, Michael, that she is a little too spirited and far too young for you."

"Thanks Mother," said Michael, "I see you don't approve of my choice either."

"Well, I have to say that she has already caused some upset in the family, so I am concerned," she replied.

"Well," said Michael, "You can all go to hell. She will be my wife and let that be an end to it." He stormed off, and the others had no doubt that he would head for the hotel.

Michael could not be deterred from his course, and Michael and Agnes were married.

1867 Hesket

Charlotte was not feeling herself. She had always tried to remain neutral about all the family bickering. She loved Robert dearly but couldn't help feeling anxious and a little angry when he fought with Michael and did little to try to solve any of the family disputes. Indeed, he often added fuel to the fire.

She was heavy with child, her fifth, and was uncharacteristically lamenting her lot in life. She glanced around her at the basic amenities that the large family shared. In the corner stood the cot, fashioned from old butter boxes. The same cot all of her four children had spent their first months in, since her first was born in 1856.

The rest of the house was none too well appointed, either. They had built extra rooms on and there were now stone chimneys at each end of the house. Timber flooring had replaced the earthen floors. But they were still sleeping on ticking mattresses and cooking was still over the open fire. They did at least have a decent table and chairs now that could accommodate the whole family. Well, the whole family when Robert actually came in from his horses or his visits to the pub in time for dinner.

Of course, they had the property in Melbourne. Charlotte had been delighted when Robert had come back from a trip to Melbourne with the news that he had brought them a city residence. Robert had brought the home in the same street as Charles, where George and Susannah had also bought a home. It would be such a relief to be able to stay in their own Melbourne residence when they visited the city, rather than having to stay with Charles.

"When can we go to have a look?" she had asked Robert excitedly.

"We will go down soon," he had replied.

When they did venture to Melbourne to see the new residence, Charlotte had been so taken with the new brick home. She could hardly believe it.

"It is beautiful, Robert," she said enthusiastically. But Robert was not particularly excited about the purchase. It was just a convenience for him, so that he had somewhere of his own to stay when he was in Melbourne on business. And, of course, it was an excellent investment as well now that the city was growing so quickly, and property prices were skyrocketing.

Charlotte had been disappointed, though. Robert was much happier working on the farm than in the city business, so they spent very little time at the new Melbourne residence.

Charlotte wished she could convince Robert to spend more money on their Hesket home. Whilst Robert and Charles were making a good living, much of the money was being spent on Robert's horse breeding program. He had brought very expensive bloodstock from England. And of course, along with horse breeding and racing, came drinking and gambling.

She could not help but think of her sister-in-law, Jane, in Melbourne with Charles. They had the best of everything in their fine city home. She thought of the fine china and ornate silver ware, the oak furniture that they had imported from England. The chintz drapes at the windows. Why couldn't she have some of these fine things?

Of course, Charles and Jane had no children and it seemed there never would. But Charles had really prospered. Robert should have the same income as he was a partner in the Melbourne business.

She rose from her chair, where she had been taking a small respite from her household duties. She could not sit for too long. It was almost dinnertime and the children would soon be coming in and they would be starving, of course. She wondered if tonight would be a good time to have a chat with Robert.

Robert appeared on time for dinner, which was a good start. After the children were all fed and getting ready for bed, she sat down by the fire with Robert.

"Robert," she said hesitantly.

"Yes, my dear, what is it?" replied Robert.

He seemed in a good mood, so now was the time to broach the subject.

"Robert, we need some things around the house. You know the baby is due soon. Could we not afford a cot and some blankets? And our own bedding is very shabby as well."

Robert's eyes showed his concern, but also there was a hint of anger as he answered.

"Really, Charlotte, you know I have been working very hard to build up my horse breeding program. We can't afford a lot of luxuries at this point."

Charlotte decided that for once she must push her point. She had sat back for too long and allowed Robert to fritter away much of their earnings.

"I understand that, Robert, and I certainly know how hard you have worked, but surely we don't need to live like paupers. You are making good money from the business in Melbourne and the sheep are doing well. We had a good deal of wool from the last shearing. Surely, we can afford a few comforts. And really, I am not asking for luxuries, as you call them. They are just ordinary things that most people of our means would expect to have."

"Oh, so you are concerned that we are not keeping a home appropriate to our standing in the community?"

"No, Robert, that is not my only concern. Although I know that you have always liked to keep up appearances. You have never let anyone know how you came to the colony. You like to be seen as a gentleman of substance. But apart from that, I work very hard too and I just think a few comforts would be appropriate."

"Very well Charlotte, said Robert frowning. I will see what we can afford when the wool cheque comes in."

Charlotte could tell that although Robert was starting to see her point of view, he was not particularly pleased that she had pushed the point. She smiled and bent over to kiss his cheek before getting up to make sure the children were all tucked into bed.

Chapter Ten

1869 Newham

John and his family had prospered in the ten years since setting up their new home and farm in Newham. They were very well respected in their new community. Harold Langdon and Grace became firm friends and the friendship had blossomed into marriage. John and his brother-in-law, Harold, became close allies and good friends. Both were god-fearing young men with strong values.

John was visiting his parents and sipped a cup of tea as he listened idly to them discussing their good fortune.

"John, you were right to convince us to move to Newham," said Rose. "It has worked out very well for our family."

"Yes, it was an excellent decision. We are thrilled that both you and Grace have made such appropriate matches too," said Samuel.

"Well, I am glad you both approve," said John with a smile. "However, not everything has gone exactly to plan. It is very disappointing that William Adams has finally gotten his hands on the remainder of the Hanging Rock land. You heard he purchased it from Alexander Archer, didn't you Father?"

"Yes, son, that is rather disturbing news."

"It would have been so much better if the Government had repurchased the land."

Samuel's brow creased.

"If only we could have more influence in how the land is used. Not that I am against all the improvements that William has made at the rock. It is looking very picturesque with the carriageway up to the summit of the rock and the new trees he has planted."

"I am not so sure about the dam across the creek to make the lake though," said John. "I am sure the bevy of swans also create a pretty picture but what will that do to our water supply I wonder. The land around the picnic grounds already has areas that can only be described as swamps. Diverting the creek could have consequences that William has not foreseen. And now he has set himself up as a publican, of course. The new Hanging Rock hotel will no doubt bring him plenty of revenue for the booths at the Sports Days."

John went quiet as memories of the first expanded New Year's Eve carnival came back to him.

The day dawned fine and hot. Excitement in the community was palpable. The first expanded carnival was planned for New Year's Day, 1866. The Sports Club had advertised the event far and wide, including in the big city newspapers. People converged from all over the countryside to enjoy the first horse races to be held at the new Hanging Rock racecourse. Since the opening of the Woodend line, the crowds from Melbourne visiting the Hanging Rock reserve had grown. So today an enormous crowd was expected. Enterprising locals made a few pounds by yoking up their draught horses to their drays and travelling to the railway station. There the draught horses waited patiently under the shade of the huge spreading snow gum for the train to steam into the station. The drays carried up to fifty people and the race goers gladly paid the price asked by the locals to get to the carnival grounds.

Locals from all the surrounding towns walked, rode, or harnessed their jinkers and buggies. They were all dressed in their Sunday best, fancy hats with wide brims decorated with flowers and feathers for the ladies, and shiny top hats and bowlers for the men. The men wore comfortable loose fitting cotton sac suits. The ladies' dresses were in a variety of colours and styles. Fabrics such as shiny chintz and cool cotton. The full skirts were gathered at the waist and fell to the ground, some with bustles. They had tightly laced bodices which were decorated with lace and buttons. On festive occasions such as this, there was a lot of colour. Most of the ladies carried parasols as protection against the scorching sun and palm-leaf fans to keep them cool.

All over the grounds, groups of people gathered around their picnic baskets. Many found their way to the publicans' booths. The day was a tremendous success. The younger set contested sack races. Young men who fancied their athletic prowess lined up for the running races. William Adams had come up with the wild idea to race geese towing tubs across the lake. The crowd found this novelty event entertaining and many bets were placed on the races. The first horse races were run on the new track.

It had been a grand day for all concerned and John knew the organisers had profited substantially from the gambling and publicans' booths. The racecourse was, however, still very rough. Despite the best efforts of William Adams at providing an improved and safer racecourse, there were still a lot of towering gum trees in close proximity to the track. These presented a dangerous risk to both horses and jockeys.

John was brought out of his reverie when his father spoke.

"Well, John, we have more important things to think about at the moment," said Samuel. "The opening of our new church is due to happen this Sunday."

Most important in the lives of the family was their devotion to the church. The Baptist congregation had continued to grow and they decided they must have a proper place of worship. They needed to build a church.

John and Samuel approached Pastor Ward on his next visit to Newham.

"Pastor, we very much appreciate that you travel all this way from Melbourne to deliver services to our congregation. We really need to build a church."

The Pastor looked at the two men.

"I agree Samuel," he said. "But it would be a huge undertaking. For a start, we don't have any land."

"That is what I wanted to speak to you about," said Samuel. "I would like to donate a piece of my land on which we could build the church."

"That is exceedingly generous of you, Samuel. Are you sure?"

"Certainly. I have thought about it for some time now. And my family should make this contribution to the church." John nodded his assent.

"Well, the congregation will certainly be very grateful to you both. We must start planning for the building."

Together, Samuel and John decided on the land that the family would donate to the church, a prominent spot on the curve of the road. Pastor Ward had been a builder in London and, besides his duties with the church, he was a contractor in Melbourne. So, of course, he was the perfect person to lead the building project. The Baptist community planned how the building would be erected. Everyone believed that it should be imposing and built to last. Pastor Ward told John that he felt sure that they could make the bricks from the clay from the nearby creek bed. It was a huge undertaking for the small Baptist community, but their faith was important to them, so John had no doubt that they would manage. They built the brick molds from timber offcuts and after they had mixed the clay with sand and water to a good consistency, they poured it into the molds. Once the bricks were dry enough to keep their shape, they carted them to the makeshift kiln for firing. It was a long and laborious process, but they were truly committed and soon the church became a reality nestled in the shadow of Hanging Rock.

Such an important new building needed to have an official opening, so soon the congregation was planning a full day of events to open the church. The day arrived when the first service was to be held in the new church. It was September 19, 1869.

The Pastor stood at the lectern. He surveyed the proud congregation and began his address.

"We owe a great debt to Samuel Marlowe and his family for the most generous donation of the land on which our church stands," He told the assembled worshippers. "We have all labored to make the bricks with which we built this church and it will stand as a symbol of our faith for many years to come."

John glanced around him at the small congregation standing proudly in their new church and celebrating their hard work.

That afternoon, several members of the congregation were baptised, including Grace and her husband Harold Langdon. The congregation made their way down to the creek following the church service to witness the baptisms.

In turn, they made their solemn commitments.

"I profess my faith in the Lord Jesus Christ and will follow him for the rest of my life," they intoned as they entered the water.

As the water rose to their waists, they dipped below the surface until their bodies were fully immersed, as was the custom in the Particular Baptist church. As they emerged from the water, still icy from the winter months, they wrapped themselves in blankets and warmed themselves at the small fire that had been lit beside the creek. Once all the baptisms had taken place, they all headed to their homes to get warm and dry and prepare for the evening's celebrations.

That evening there was a ball at the Newham Hall. The ladies dressed in their finery. They delighted in the opportunity to leave their farm clothes behind and don their best gowns. They all carried baskets filled to the brim with all sorts of delicacies for a delicious supper. The local brass band played the music for dancing. The older members watched on and the children darted around in between the legs of the adults.

It had been a long, proud day for this committed group of pioneers.

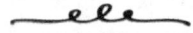

1870 Hanging Rock

Samuel and John Marlowe, together with Harold Langdon, had become the fiercest campaigners for the appropriate use of Hanging Rock and the surrounding land, and they were not alone. Many other farmers supported their protests.

The Hanging Rock Sports Carnivals were being held regularly on New Year's Day, but also now on other holidays such as Boxing Day. Each year, the events grew and expanded. Not that the farmers necessarily opposed these events. In fact, many of them attended the Carnival days. But John, Samuel and Harold, as members of the Baptist community, objected to the gambling that accompanied the horse racing, and as a temperate religion, they also opposed the indulgence in alcohol. The crowds always became rowdy and unruly towards the end of the long, hot carnival days.

Once again, the three men discussed the problem of the reserve.

"This situation is not improving," said Harold. "I ran into Robert Blayney last week. I took the cattle over to the creek and he was training his horses at the racecourse. He really is a pompous old fool. He wanted an argument, telling me I had no right to have the cattle at the creek. Yet he thinks he had the right to train his horses anytime he likes. And I am sure he had been drinking."

"I know what you mean Harold," said John. "The whole family seems to be a law unto themselves. I suppose William Adams tolerates him on the racecourse because he makes a tidy profit from horse racing."

"Well, at least we have had a partial win now that the land the Government retained has been formally gazetted," said Samuel. "Those letters that I wrote to the Council and Minister of Lands had little effect. Fortunately, the petition seems to have made the difference."

"Yes, I agree," said Harold. "It was a lot of work getting the signatures, but it was worth it. I think the name of Hanging Rock Recreation and Water Reserve is important as well. It makes it clear to everyone that farmers have a right to access the water."

"It is pleasing to know that at least that area won't fall into the wrong hands now," added Samuel.

"Yes, but it doesn't solve the problem Father," said John. "The Rock itself is still in private hands."

Samuel, John, and Harold decided it was time to approach William Adams with their concerns. Samuel, being the patriarch of the family, cleared his throat and made the first approach.

"William, we appreciate the improvements you have made to the rock and surrounds. The picnic ground and the lake are looking wonderful. However, we have concerns."

"Yes," continued John. "It's about our access to the land. We have always been able to water our stock here."

"I do not see your problem. There is no one stopping you from accessing the land," said William. "We only hold the sports meetings on a select few days each year and every other day you are free to water your cattle. In fact, I see your stock roaming free all the time. But remember, I own a good portion of this land. It is only through my generosity that you have been allowed to access the water via my land. By rights, you should only have your stock on the reserve. I would be keeping quiet if I were you."

However, this did not satisfy the trio. They decided that more needed to be done.

"We need to convince the Government to repurchase the other 170 acres," said John. "It is the only right way to proceed."

"But what more can we do?" asked Harold.

"Newham Shire Council elections are coming up soon," said John. "I think I should stand. We need better representation."

"That is a wonderful idea, John," enthused his father. "You are the perfect man for the job with your even temper and clear thinking. I think you could do some real good."

Harold heartily agreed. As it happened, John's quest to become a councillor eventuated sooner than expected. One of the sitting councillors had an horrific accident and, sadly, died. He had been a very popular and proactive councillor so John would have big shoes to fill. But everyone in the community thought he was up to the task. The Marlowe family felt that at last they could make some actual progress in their lobbying to the Government.

The Government placed control of the newly gazetted reserve in the hands of the Newham Shire Council. And because the Council had been handed management of the land, some of the Councillors decided that it might be a good idea to fence the reserve, so they could lease the land out, which of course added further fuel to the flames. The farmers were immediately up in arms.

At a fiery council meeting, John Marlowe stood to address the meeting.

"What of these plans to fence the Recreation and Water Reserve? The very idea of the reserve is that access should remain open to anyone who chooses to use it," said John

Immediately, another councillor rose. He was a well-known horse breeder, a friend of Robert Blayney, and so, of course, was very much in favour of racing and sports meetings being held at the rock.

"Well, we need to have some control of who accesses the reserve and we also need to be able to close off the area for sports meetings."

The argument raged on.

John watched as Harold galloped towards him. As he dismounted, John could see that his friend was fuming. Harold's face was ruddy and his eyes blazed.

"John, that man has gone completely mad," he said. "He has just threatened me with his shillelagh."

"Who are you referring to?" asked John calmly. He knew his friend well enough to know that he would need to stay quiet and allow Harold to relate his story.

"William Adams. I have just been to the spring to get water. He told me to get off his land. It seems he would have had blood on his hands, rather than let me have a drop of water. He is usually an even-tempered man. I am not sure what I did to rile him up that much."

"This is getting out of hand," said John. "We must continue to pursue the Government to buy back the land."

"I am going to write to the Council again," raged Harold. "Adams should not be allowed to get away with this. I will demand to know why he barred me when I know other local families are accessing the water."

"That seems like a good idea, Harold," replied John. "I think William is feeling the strain of all the conflict that has surrounded his land. And he knows that you have been one of the most vocal opponents of private ownership. You will do yourself no favours with your anger though. Your letter should calmly relate the facts. And I can talk to it at the council meeting. I actually think that if we could get the government to agree to buy back the land, William would happily sell it."

Chapter Eleven

1875 Hesket

When 80 year old Harriet became critically ill, Charles came back to the farm for an extended period to be at her side. The local doctor came regularly to check on her. But there was nothing he could do. He told the family that her heart was giving out and that she didn't have long to live. All her family gathered around her. They took turns sitting at her bedside for many days as she slowly deteriorated.

Before the end, she asked to speak to Robert and Charles alone. Charles was not really surprised that she had not asked Michael to join them. And as for George, he had distanced himself from the family, so there was really no point including him either. Charles knew it saddened his mother that George and Susannah rarely visited the farm now, having handed over most of the responsibility to other family members. But Charles also knew that the family bickering was the main reason George stayed away and he could certainly understand that.

Harriet tried to lift herself up. Charles hurried forward to help her and arrange the pillows behind her head.

"My darling boys," she said. "I know I do not have much time left and I am going to join your father." This thought brought a small smile to her face.

"Oh Mother, please don't talk like that," said Charles, although he knew her remaining time was short. Robert stood quietly at Charles's side, not saying anything, his anxiety showing clearly on his face.

"It is the truth, Charles. There is no use denying it. But there is something I want you both to do. I do not know what will become of Rebecca when I am gone. She has been so good to me and I am worried about her. George is rarely here now and she and Michael have never gotten along. They both have tempers that they struggle to control. You boys must both promise me you will look after her. She will need you both."

"Of course, Mother," said Charles. "We will take care of her." Robert just nodded. Despite his tough exterior, Charles could see that Robert was struggling to control his emotions and voice his feelings as their mother was fading.

Not many more days passed before she took her last breath. They buried her in the same plot as they buried their father 22 years earlier.

All of her children and grandchildren surrounded the grave as the minister said final prayers and the coffin was lowered into the ground.

Charles and Robert stood on either side of Rebecca. George stood close by. But Charles noticed Michael was standing well back from the rest of the family with Agnes. Rebecca's tears flowed freely as she threw a handful of dirt onto her mother's coffin. She was devastated by Harriet's death, having been her mother's constant companion for as long as they could all remember.

Rebecca never married. Charles knew that her mother depended heavily on her after Albert died. Harriet had missed him dreadfully, and Rebecca put most of her efforts into trying to make her mother happy. Despite her fiery disposition, Rebecca cared deeply for her mother and Charles knew she would have done anything for her.

Chapter Twelve

1880 Hanging Rock

The Marlowe family gathered at Samuel's grand home on New Year's Day. In recent years, the house had seen many renovations and expansions. Several more rooms had been added, built from stone quarried from the land and now an iron roof was in place. New furniture graced the sitting room. There were comfortable chairs with well-stuffed cushions, along with side tables bearing beautiful ornaments. They now ate and drank from fine china and crystal glasses.

The entire extended family was gathered to celebrate the start of the year of 1880. They sat on the verandah, as it was the coolest part of the house. All were dressed in their best clothes as today was a holiday and there would be no work on the farm. The women sat quietly, occupied with their fine needlework. John glanced around and smiled as he took in the happy family scene. He was thankful that he, his father and his brother-in-law Harold had so much in common. Whilst his entire family were staunch in their religious beliefs, he knew that the three of them had strong principles and felt strongly about the need to uphold their duties as civic-minded people and members of the church.

John looked out over the paddocks at the potato crop. Over the years, Samuel and John both developed a fascination for potatoes and experimented with many varieties in the fertile soil. There was now also a wheat crop. A flour mill had started operations in Newham and the local farmers had all planted wheat to ensure that there was plenty of flour for bread making. The cattle were thriving and the flock of sheep was growing. Lambing season had gone well that year. His father's fruit trees were also doing well. Samuel grew pears and plums which he sent to Melbourne to preserving factories. John also had plum trees on his farm, which added to the crop sent to Melbourne.

From where they sat on the verandah, they could see the crowds converging on the carnival grounds. Sometimes they would attend the Hanging Rock Sports Carnival in the early part of the day, but they always left before it became too rowdy. Today, they had decided to spend the day at home. It was a burning hot day, and they all knew the hotter the day, the more the racegoers would drink and the better business would be for the publicans' booths.

"Looks like they are in for a big day," said John.

"Yes, it is going to get very hot, so there will be gallons of alcohol consumed and a lot of money will no doubt change hands in the betting rings," said Harold.

They watched on as the ever-increasing crowds became more raucous by the hour and bemoaned the fact that their neighbours felt the need to drink and carry on with such abandon and to gamble their hard-earned money on horses racing around in circles. "What are we going to do about this?" Samuel asked the younger men. "This is not how the community should use our wonderful reserve."

"It is upsetting, Father," said John. "We need to keep lobbying. I haven't given up yet."

Robert Blayney was the Clerk of the Course for this Hanging Rock Sports Day. He swelled with importance as he surveyed his surroundings. He was resplendent in his race day attire. His shiny top hat hid his greying hair and shaded his eyes from the burning summer sun. Although his three-piece suit was made of light cotton, he knew it would be a day where he would need to keep his liquid consumption up. He stood chatting with a group of racing club officials, who included the stewards, the starter and the Judge.

"It looks like we will have a sensational crowd today," he said to his fellow officials.

"Yes, I think this will be one of the best yet," replied Mr Savage, who was officiating as the starter.

Together they surveyed the enormous crowd and the carnival like atmosphere that surrounded them. Once again this year, thousands of people were descending on the reserve to enjoy themselves with the variety of entertainment that the day presented.

The crowds had continued to grow each year as people travelled from even further afield, including a large number from Melbourne. Many fine carriages were lined up at the entry. The roads were much improved, so many drove their own carriages these days. The locals from the surrounding towns of Hesket, Lancefield, Romsey, Woodend and Newham were also arriving in large numbers. As usual, along with the horse races, there were foot races, long jump competitions and other novelty events. The local crack shots took part in the shooting competitions. Young bucks who fancied themselves as runners assembled for the foot races. And this year, for the first time, the ladies could compete in the 50 yard running race. Prizes for the events were small but highly sought after. The number of publicans' booths had also grown, as had the stalls selling all types of local produce. The vibrant sounds of local bands and minstrels filled the air. Racegoers and picnickers came for a day of enjoyment and frivolity as a break from their otherwise tedious and hardworking lives.

Today, the first ever Hanging Rock Cup would be run, and the inaugural horse race was to be a spectacular and exciting event for all. There was a £15 prize for the winner. Robert had one of his thoroughbred horses running in the event, but he knew he had stiff competition. Edward Dryden, known for his expertise in the judgement of horseflesh, had entered his horse, Commodore. Robert took some time out from his official duties to see that his horse and jockey were ready to race.

"How is he looking?" Robert asked the young bloke who was riding his horse, Flame, named for the bright chestnut of his coat.

"He is fired up and ready to run," replied the jockey as he brushed the sleek coat of the beautiful animal.

Robert rubbed the horse's nose and then hurried back to his post to watch the race. He looked out over the racecourse. It was short and looped around some large gums with tight corners. It was still considered to be a dangerous racecourse, where in previous years several jockeys had come to grief. Fortunately, there had been no serious mishaps so far. Some jockeys worried that someone would be hurt badly if the racecourse was not improved. Robert thought about the plans being hatched by the Hanging Rock Sports Club to extend the racecourse and make other improvements such as more publicans' booths. It was going to take some careful negotiations to get the more conservative sections of the community to agree.

The excitement built as the riders and horses trotted into the mounting yard for the Hanging Rock Cup. They moved out onto the track and assembled at the starting line. The crack of the starting gun echoed around the rock and the horses were away. Flame made a good start, but it was soon clear that Commodore was the horse to beat. As they thundered along the track, Commodore found a gap and raced to the front, beating the other horses by two lengths. Robert's horse had not placed, but he was relieved that there had been no mishaps. Commodore was led back to the mounting yard and Dryden was awarded with the inaugural Hanging Rock Cup and the £15 prize.

Robert strode up to Dryden.

"Congratulations Edward," he said. "But you know I will have a horse that will beat you one day."

Dryden laughed. "I rather doubt it, Robert, but thanks anyway. My horse is a real beauty."

As the day wore on, the sweltering heat increased and so did the amount of alcohol that was consumed. Robert certainly had his fair share.

After a fairly successful day, Robert mounted his horse and headed for home. Despite his horse not winning the cup, he had won a small wad of cash in the betting ring. His sense of importance at being Clerk of the Course was somewhat inflated by the liquor he had consumed.

As he was riding home along a narrow track through swampy ground near the creek, he met some fellow race goers. Given his inebriated state, he took objection to them being in his path.

"Move!" He yelled indignantly to the young man he knew as Reid. Reid, however, stood his ground so as not to be forced into the surrounding swamp.

"There is room for you to pass, Blayney," Reid retorted. "I am not getting my boots wet and muddy by moving off the track, you arrogant prig." It was apparent that Reid had also consumed his share of intoxicating drink during the long hot day, increasing his bravado.

Robert raised his whip and struck the young man with the butt. Reid stared at Robert in disbelief. It was clear that he had not expected to be struck. Reid grabbed at the bridle of Robert's horse. The startled horse reared and Robert was thrown to the ground. Though he was an accomplished horseman, he was none too steady on his mount. As he picked himself up, he roared at Reid.

"You will pay for this, young man."

Just then, the local constable rode up on his horse.

"Can I be of any assistance here?" he asked. He knew Robert well.

Reid accused Robert of running him off the track into the swamp and assaulting him with his whip. In his turn, Robert complained to the constable that Reid had caused his horse to rear and throw him off.

"This young man needs to show more respect," blustered Robert.

"Well, it seems to me this will need to be sorted out at the station. I am charging you both with public affray. You will hear from me."

Both Reid and Robert felt the most prudent course of action was to move on.

1880 Melbourne

As prosperity from the gold rush and sheep exports saw Melbourne burgeon into a city of great wealth, Charles's standing in the community also grew.

Charles's office reflected his increased stature in Melbourne and as he glanced at a portrait of himself in his council robes, he reflected on his years since arriving in the ever-expanding city. Upon his arrival in Australia, he had quickly realised that this was a land of opportunity. When he first came to Melbourne 25 years ago, the city was in its infancy. The slums of Little Lon and the inner city did not attract him. He had purchased a tract of land in West Melbourne across from what was now the Flagstaff Gardens. He could well remember those early days when he had worked hard to build his reputation as a well-to-do gentleman. Making the money had been relatively easy. The gold rush had seen to that. The carting business had paid huge dividends. He was now a very wealthy man. But the difficulty had been in establishing himself in the circles of the upper echelon of Melbourne society. Especially given his two brothers were ex-convicts and the escapades of his family back in Hesket often made the pages of the city newspapers. That he had achieved his goal was a source of great pride for him.

Charles had a distinguished air about him these days, no longer the revolutionary of his youth, having recently celebrated his 62nd birthday. His hair was completely grey and he sported a bushy grey beard, as was the fashion of the day. His face showed the wrinkles of his age, but his eyes were clear and bright.

He had used some of his substantial wealth to assist him in rising up the ranks of the rich and famous, making significant contributions to worthy causes, such as the children's hospital. It never hurt to grease a few palms in order to raise one's profile. He made the most of any opportunity to demonstrate that he was a community minded entrepreneur. When a vacancy had opened up for the Bourke Ward of the Melbourne Corporation, due to a resignation, he stood as a candidate and was elected as a councillor. There was nothing Charles enjoyed more than dressing up in his satiny council garb, complete with lace jabot, to attend council meetings where he could mix with the elite. He also took on the role of Secretary of the West Melbourne Literacy Institute, a circulating library and reading room.

This year, 1880, was to be the year of the Melbourne International Exhibition, and he was one of the commissioners responsible for bringing this monumental event to fruition. It was an exciting and daunting project. But now that the work was almost complete, Charles was very much looking forward to the grand opening in October.

Of course, Charles had worked extremely hard to build his business interests here in Melbourne, but he supposed he should thank Robert for some of his good fortune. If Robert hadn't gone off prospecting for gold, the family would not have had the chance to amass so much wealth. And whilst Robert's primary interest had always been in his horse breeding program back in Hesket, he had been a solid business partner, despite his fiery and somewhat erratic disposition. The two brothers made a good team.

But Charles had other thoughts on his mind this morning. His troublesome family was once again in need of his support. Robert had been charged with public affray at the New Year's Day races and would have to face court. His wayward brother Michael and his family continued to cause trouble. Michael's wife, Agnes, was continually bickering with the other members of the family. He would need to take a trip to Hesket to sort it all out.

That evening, after a busy day dealing with council matters, he broached the subject with his wife, Jane. Whilst she supported him, she retained her calm and did not enter into any of the family squabbles. He was very thankful for that.

"They are at it again, Jane," he said. "Can you believe it?"

"Unfortunately, I would believe anything your family might get up to, Charles," Jane replied. "I must say their petty behaviour has become very tiresome."

Charles explained all the recent dramas that were unfolding in Hesket.

"We must make the journey down there to see if we can sort it out."

"Of course, Charles, if that is what you think is necessary."

The next day, they prepared to travel. Charles's wealth and position meant that they had access to a comfortable carriage and a good pair of horses to make the journey. Fortunately, the roads had improved over the past 10 years. But it was still an onerous journey.

Eventually, tired and somewhat disheveled, they reached the farm. The intention was not to make contact with any of the family until they had had a chance to recover from the journey. But no sooner had they settled into their farmhouse than Robert was on the doorstep.

"Thank goodness you have finally deigned to grace us with your presence," said a disgruntled Robert. "Michael and Agnes are causing problems again. Hello Jane," he added, almost as an afterthought.

"It's all very well for you, in your ivory tower in the city, but I am here having to sort it all out."

"Settle down," said Charles. "I am here now and we can see what I can do. And anyway, what about you causing problems at the races? When is your court date?"

"Oh well, that was not my fault. That crazy young Reid should have known better than to confront me in the way he did. Young people do not know how to show respect to someone in my position. I am sure the court will see it my way."

"Oh really? Well, I hope you are right. When is it?"

"It is on Monday in Woodend. But let's get back to Michael and Agnes," said Robert. "They are running down the farm. Michael is drinking constantly. Agnes and Rebecca are continually bickering. I am at my wit's end trying to deal with it all."

"Alright, I can see that you are upset. Let's pay them a visit and see what they are up to. Perhaps we can offer to help out on the farm."

1880 Hesket

As Charles and Robert approached the cottage, they could hear raised voices.

Michael and Agnes had been married for 16 years. It had been a turbulent marriage from the beginning. The two of them fought constantly. Michael seemed determined to make up for time lost whilst he was incarcerated by spending many hours in the Hanging Rock Hotel. He came home drunk on many an evening.

"You are drunk again," said Agnes. "Why do you have to come home in this state every night? There is work to be done. I can't do everything. Can't you at least come home in time for dinner?"

"Well, why would I want to be here?" Michael replied. "You are always nagging me and finding fault with everything I do."

"If you were ever here, that would be true, but I don't see how I can nag you when you are not here. The farm is not doing well and your family is constantly at my throat trying to get you to pick up your game and do some work to pull things back into shape. Look at the sheep. They don't look after themselves, you know. Have you arranged the shearers yet?"

The entire conversation was audible to Charles and Robert through the open window as they approached the cottage.

Charles knocked firmly on the door. An obviously angry Agnes opened the door. She rolled her eyes and groaned.

Agnes had given birth to seven children, and another was on the way. Despite still being a young woman, the strain of her life showed in the premature lines on her face.

"What do you want?" asked Agnes.

"Aren't you going to invite us in, Agnes?" asked Charles courteously. Robert, on the other hand, glowered at his sister-in-law.

Agnes turned and yelled over her shoulder. "Your brothers are here, Michael."

The brothers entered the room and at once Charles understood what Robert had been worrying about. The room was a hovel and Charles could immediately tell that Michael was really in no fit state to have a sensible conversation. He sat sullenly in the corner and had not yet said a word to his brothers.

However, Charles decided he needed to at least try to talk to his brother.

"Hello Michael," said Charles jovially, determined to keep the conversation light. "It's good to see you. How are you?"

"How do you think I am?" responded Michael.

"Well, I can see that you seem a little out of sorts. Look Michael, Robert and I just want to help. We can see the farm needs a bit of work. Can we help you organise the shearers?"

"Well, somebody needs to do something," said Agnes. "You can see the state of the place. I can't do it all on my own."

"That's rich coming from you," said Michael. "Look at this mess."

"How dare you! I have the children to take care of. I need more help. You are never here, always at the pub and coming home at all hours in no fit state to do anything."

Agnes was not keen on hard work herself, and the house and farm were unkempt and the animals in a poor state.

Charles could see their attempts to try to help were not going to work, whilst Michael and Agnes were so angry. So, the brothers took their leave.

"Well, what exactly to you propose we do about them?" asked Robert as they walked back to their farms.

"I am sure I don't know, Robert, but I must get back to Melbourne as soon as possible after your court hearing. I have the opening of the Melbourne Exhibition to attend. It will be a monumental event."

Robert was not impressed. He no longer had any interest in his brother's climb up the Melbourne social ladder. Despite having a residence in Melbourne and being a partner in the business, Robert was becoming increasingly withdrawn from the fancy city scene and spent very little time there.

The following Monday, the two brothers fronted up at the Woodend Court House. Robert was called to give evidence first.

"This young man knocked me from my horse. I have a bruise and a cut on my forehead where I hit the ground. And I also have the shirt that I was wearing. You can see the blood."

Mr Geake, appearing for the defendant, Reid, stated that there was no case. "It is simply, as Shakespeare puts it, 'Man dressed in little brief authority, what a tyrant he becomes'." Robert Blayney had been officiating as Clerk of the Course and had made himself particularly obnoxious and assaulted my client with no provocation."

Despite this speech, the bench elected to hear the evidence for the defence. Senior Constable Waters took the stand.

"I saw Robert strike Reid with the butt end of his whip. I did not see Reid retaliate, although I do believe he may have grabbed the reins of Blayney's horse."

After issuing Robert with a fine, the judge adjourned the case and the gallery stood as he left the courtroom.

Robert and his family left the court with Robert blustering that the law was an ass. "How can we expect to receive justice in this town?" he raged.

"Settle down, Robert," said Charles. "Let that be an end to it. If you keep getting yourself into trouble, you cannot expect the court to be on your side."

Robert glared at him but said no more.

1880 Melbourne

Charles assisted his wife, Jane, into their handsome carriage and then climbed in beside her. Jane was elegantly turned out for this auspicious occasion. Charles himself was dressed in his council robes. He smiled at his beautiful wife. As usual, she looked stunning. She was wearing a well-tailored emerald green gown with a tightly fitted bodice and a high lace neckline. The full skirt was gathered at her waist and was complete with a bustle at the back. She wore a wide-brimmed hat trimmed with a delicate bouquet of flowers. Her feet were clad in dainty boots with a neat heel. To complete the outfit, she wore a diamond necklace around her neck, a gift from Charles to mark the occasion. It was Friday October 1, and the Government had declared a public holiday to mark the occasion of the Opening of the 1880 Melbourne International Exhibition.

The driver whipped up the finely bred horses and the carriage drove away from their Jeffcott Street home on route to the Exhibition Buildings on the other side of the city. As they travelled down Lonsdale Street, they were amazed at the enormous crowds that had flocked to the city. People hoping to get a good view of the procession lined Swanston and Spring Streets. Charles knew there would be thousands assembled at the best vantage points on the steps of the Treasury Building and Parliament House. Flags of every description flew on all the major buildings.

Luckily, they had arrived in plenty of time, so when they alighted from the carriage at the entrance, they were able to make their way into the building without impediment. Charles escorted his wife to her seat and then made his way to his seat, nodding acknowledgment to the other Commissioners.

Charles, as a Councillor of the City of Melbourne, had felt great pride when he had been appointed as a Commissioner for the Exhibition.

The Commissioners had only had two years to pull all this together. They were charged with the onerous task of organising the construction of the new Exhibition Building and the running of the International Exhibition of Works and Industries of Art. As he sat waiting for the formalities to get underway, Charles breathed out audibly. He thought back to that appointment and remembered wondering how they could possibly make this happen in the short time frame. However, plans for the new Exhibition Building in the Carlton Gardens were soon drawn up and the foundation stone was laid early in 1879 by the then Governor of Victoria, His Excellency, Sir George Bowen. Charles and the other commissioners had worked diligently to ensure this tremendous event, with exhibitors from all over the world, was a success. He had served on three committees, one of which was the building committee. So, he, of course, had been heavily involved in appointing the architect and overseeing the construction of the new Exhibition Building. Costs had blown out, as more space became necessary to accommodate the unexpected demand for exhibition space from the many international exhibitors from all corners of the globe. However, the Exhibition Building now stood as a monument to the wealth and prosperity of Melbourne.

Marvellous Melbourne, as it had now become known, had pulled off this amazing display of industry and arts, thanks to the gold rush and wool industry boom which the whole of Victoria had been experiencing for around thirty years. The city's wealth meant that the Commissioners had spared no expense.

Charles looked around as he waited for the official party to arrive. He was seated in the great hall beneath the dome. The pavilions stretched out on all sides. It was indeed an imposing and impressive sight. The exhibits were an amazing display of industry and riches. Dignitaries from all over the world, as well as the Governors of each of the Australian colonies, were assembled, resplendent in highly decorated military uniforms and formal dress. In front of him, he could see the huge organ pipes and assembled in front of the pipes was the choir. They were all dressed in white except for their colourful sashes, which differentiated the sections. The orchestra was assembled, ready to begin.

Outside, the participants in the procession, which included trades organisations, military battalions, firemen and bands, would be converging from all over the city, walking proudly behind their colourful banners. At the Swanston Street corner, they would await the arrival of the Governor and his entourage from Government House, and then the procession would continue down Flinders Street before turning into Spring Street and proceeding to the main entrance of the Exhibition Building.

Finally, it was time. Charles straightened in his seat as the sound of the military band announced the arrival of the Governor and the vice regal party. As the party ascended the dais, all stood for the playing of the national anthem, God Save the Queen, followed by three rousing cheers. The assembly then took their seats again for the performance of the cantata by the orchestra and choir. Charles found the hour-long performance majestic. As the music faded, His Excellency, Lord Normanby, Governor of Victoria, rose to declare the Exhibition officially open. Immediately following the opening, the gigantic gold-plated Statue of Industry was unveiled to an audible gasp from the audience.

Several months later Charles was handed a copy of the final report. He related the information from the report to Jane as they sat enjoying a nightcap on a hot summer evening.

"I am so proud, Jane," he said. "The Exhibition has been wholly satisfactory. More than a million people paid for admission. The whole event went way over budget, so we are all very relieved that much of the cost has been recouped by such good attendances. Such a successful Exhibition will open up new markets and make the colonies better known throughout the world."

1884 Woodend

As time wore on, Rebecca became increasingly bad tempered. Robert was worried about her. He had tried to look after her since their mother died, but Rebecca did not make it easy. She was constantly bickering with Michael and Agnes. She never approved of the match, thinking that Michael had married beneath himself and so she blamed Agnes for her long running dispute with Michael. Robert agreed with her that Michael's family were difficult to get along with and he did not have any time for Agnes and Michael's brood, which now numbered nine.

Now the two women found themselves in court in Woodend. Agnes had charged Rebecca with assault. Robert attended the court to give support to Rebecca, but he also secretly hoped that he would be able to keep her in line. As they entered the courthouse, Robert gave Michael and Agnes a curt nod. They all stood as the judge entered the courtroom. He opened the proceedings by reading the charges.

"Rebecca Blayney, you are hereby charged with the assault of Agnes Blayney at her home on the February 11, 1884," intoned the Judge. "What do you have to say for yourself?"

"Well, your honour, she provoked me," stated Rebecca.

"Can you tell us what happened, Mrs Blayney?" asked the judge, turning to the plaintiff, Agnes.

"Your honour, my turkeys had gone missing, and I simply went to Rebecca's place to search for them. I wouldn't put it past her to lock them up and claim them as hers. When I went to her house to ask her about them, she went completely off the handle. She came into the yard waving a great stick around in the air and she called me a strumpet! Can you believe it, a strumpet? I never gave her any provocation, and she laid into me with the stick so hard that she broke the stick."

Rebecca immediately lost her temper. "She is lying. I never so much as touched her with the stick. She came at me, accusing me of stealing her turkeys. I did no such thing. What was I supposed to do? Of course, I called her a strumpet. That is the way she behaves."

The judge leaned forward. "Please Miss Blayney, you must control yourself. We are in a court of law."

"Control myself," shouted Rebecca. "It is Agnes who should control herself. She is always blaming others for her bad fortune. I can't help it if she cannot take care of her turkeys."

"That's enough, Miss Blayney."

But Rebecca could not be calmed. Robert tried in vain, but could not stop her shouting at the judge. The judge had no alternative but to adjourn the matter.

Robert led Rebecca from the court before she could continue her yelling match with Agnes.

"Really Rebecca, you must control yourself. I know how badly you feel about Agnes but provoking her is not the answer."

"What am I supposed to do? She is unbearable. I can't believe that Michael still puts up with her."

"I know. I completely agree. She has caused nothing but trouble in our family. But there is no point in making the situation worse. Now you will have to go back to court again to resolve this matter."

"I know Robert, but she makes me so angry," said Rebecca, starting to calm down. Robert did not know what was to become of Rebecca. He had certainly noticed the deterioration of her mental state since their mother's death.

He put his arm around her shoulders and hugged her to him.

"Come on, Rebecca," he said. "Let's go home and you can make me a cup of tea."

Chapter Thirteen

1884 Newham

T he mood was volatile. Townspeople from the small set-
tlements of Hesket, Woodend and Newham were gathering in the Newham Hall. Over the last few years, the dispute
about rights to the local land and water surrounding Hanging
Rock had not abated. The meeting had been called to try again
to thrash out the arguments from both sides. The only thing
the community had ever been able to agree upon was the fact
that the Government should never have sold Hanging Rock in
the first place.

All parties were, however, pleased to note that there had
been a breakthrough. The Woodend Star had printed the
welcome news on October 11, 1884.

PURCHASE OF HANGING ROCK RESERVE

*The purchase of the well-known and attractive recreation
ground, known as Hanging Rock, Mount Macedon, was completed this week by Mr. Tucker, the Minister of Lands. The
land purchased comprises 72 acres, a short distance from
Woodend, in the parish of Newham, and adjoins a piece of
comparatively level ground of about 100 acres still in the
possession of the Crown. The two areas will therefore, form
one reserve of 172 acres, which may be fairly described as one
of the most beautiful and picturesque public reserves in the*

colony. Mr Tucker gave instructions yesterday for its perma-
nent reservation and dedication to the free use of the public
henceforward.

The value of the recreation ground now secured may be
estimated when it is considered that, although a charge was
made for admission by the proprietor, frequently from 5000 to
10,000 people have visited it on holidays, and that it is also
visited by tourists from all parts of the colony. The strange
feature is, of course, the immense and almost numberless piles
of rocks, many of them hundreds of tons in weight, that stand
together in all sorts of fantastic shapes and positions, but so
that paths between them and over them lead to the very top
of the highest, which may be reached by foot or on horseback,
from whence a splendid panoramic view is obtained of the
country for miles around.

Clear icy rills and spring water on the hottest summer day
flow and emerge from between the crevices, whilst underfoot
the ground reverberates like a drum, showing the existence of
caves, which will probably be now opened out and explored.
The Government may be congratulated upon regaining this
fine property, which it is to be hoped will never again pass
from the hands of the people.

Robert knew that William Adams had sold the land willingly. Whilst he had benefitted from ownership for many years, to
his credit, he agreed that such an important landmark should
be public property.

But despite the welcome news, Robert and the Hanging
Rock Sports Club were not content. They had decided that a
new racecourse should be built on the land. The rough track
that William Adams had set out on his land was just not safe
or appropriate for racing. The Victorian Racing Commission
was insisting that the track be made safer and amenities be
improved in order to meet new requirements. Without a new
racecourse, Robert knew that racing would not be able to
continue at Hanging Rock. The Newham Shire Council was

once again drawn into the argument about whether the land should be used for horse racing.

Local identities were divided as usual. Robert nodded grimly to John Marlowe and Harold Langdon as he and his son, Edward, entered the meeting.

"You need to get involved in this issue Edward," said Robert. "Your interest in horse breeding and racing will be affected by what becomes of the land around the Rock. If those two have their way, there will never be any more horse racing at Hanging Rock."

Edward shot his father an impatient look. Robert supposed he hardly needed to be told about the Hanging Rock dispute. He had listened to his father bemoan the happenings around this issue for years.

Robert was very proud of his good-looking son. He was well aware that Edward had little interest in ordinary farming pursuits. He wasn't that keen on too much hard work, which irked Robert somewhat, but he forgave his son this weakness, as he was the only one of his offspring who took an interest in horse breeding. And he was good at it. Robert had no doubt that Edward would make his mark as a horse breeder.

"Yes, Father, that is why I am here," Edward replied. "I know full well the importance of getting these do-gooders to allow the building of a proper racecourse."

As the hall filled, the atmosphere continued to build. Presently, John Marlowe strode purposefully to the podium. As a councillor on the Newham Shire Council, he would chair the meeting.

"Good afternoon, everyone," John said in a loud, clear voice.

"Order. Order," he continued as the noisy crowd continued to converse loudly. Slowly, the level of noise decreased.

"We are here today to discuss the Hanging Rock Recreation and Water Reserve," he began.

"I know you are all aware of the history of the Hanging Rock reserve and will also be aware that it has now come back into public hands. This is a victory for our community. So today we are here to discuss how we will all work together as a community to make the best use of the Reserve."

"Oh, we all know how you want it to be used, John Marlowe," came a voice from the crowd. A general raising of voices followed this remark as others declared what their interests were.

"Remarks such as that will not help this discussion," said John from the podium.

"Let us all take our turns to have our say in an orderly manner. As chairperson of this meeting, I would first like to ask Harold Langdon to speak on behalf of the farmers." This invitation bought jeers and derision from many of those assembled. Everyone in attendance, including Robert and Edward, knew that Harold was John's brother-in-law and would simply be voicing John's opinions. Harold approached the podium.

"You will all be aware that I have fought for many years to maintain access to the water and grazing on the reserve. In fact, on occasions, I have been physically threatened trying to access water. I cannot condone the use of our reserve, which I remind you is the property of all people, for horse racing. The idea that the Sports Club should be allowed to take up such a huge part of the land with a racecourse is just ludicrous. We must leave the land open for all. And it would be remiss of me not to mention that horse racing encourages gambling and drinking copious amounts of alcohol."

This was met by a general hubbub from the assembled audience, including cheers, but also a good smattering of derisive catcalls.

"Order," called John Marlowe as he strode to centre of the stage again. "We now have a speaker for the other side."

Robert Blayney made his way up to the podium and cleared his throat.

"We need to encourage recreation. There is nothing wrong with enjoying our very few days of rest in this harsh environment. We all work hard. Why shouldn't we have our sports and horse racing days? What is the harm in it?"

"What is the harm? Intoxicated people falling over each other and causing a ruckus. That is the harm!" This remark had come from an anonymous voice in the crowd.

Further speakers for both sides followed, but the meeting descended into chaos despite John's best efforts to maintain control.

Robert's ire was raised as he left the meeting. He felt that John and Harold had too much to say. As he walked towards his horse, he came face to face with John.

"Look here, John. This meeting was not a fair representation of both sides of the argument," he said, pointing his finger at John's chest.

"I am sorry, Robert," replied John. "But I cannot agree with you. You had your say."

"Well, I am sick of this argument. You people need to understand that horse racing and recreation are important to many people in this district."

"I must agree with you Robert. I am also sick of this argument. I would much prefer if our community could finally come to some agreement."

"It is obviously a waste of time talking to you. Just wait, we will have our new racecourse despite your one-sided opinions." Robert stormed off, joining Edward, who had been waiting patiently.

Despite the opposition from some sections of the community, and after several fiery council meetings, the decision was made to allow the racecourse to be built on the east side of the rock. The horse breeders and racing enthusiasts had won the day.

Jubilant horse racing enthusiasts then got together and formed the Hanging Rock Racing Club. Robert and Edward were among the first members of the club and worked diligently to ensure the new racecourse was built to the highest standard. The Racing Club was soon able to run the first horse races that would be officially sanctioned by the Victorian Racing Commission.

Chapter Fourteen

1888 Hanging Rock

E dward looked forward with excitement to the New Year's Day races when his fine new thoroughbred would make its debut in the Hanging Rock Cup. Now the day had finally arrived. His horse breeding program was making significant profits. So much so that he purchased a Purebred Suffolk Punch colt descended from a famous English horse. It was his pride and joy and he was sure it could win the Cup.

Racing had a strong foothold in the area now, despite the continuing opposition from some sections of the community. The new racecourse wound around the lake, providing a picturesque outlook for racegoers. The Hanging Rock Cup and the other races on the program were now very much the focal point of the day. Of course, the publicans' booths were still well supported and a carnival atmosphere prevailed.

As the crowd built, Edward's excitement grew. His horse was standing patiently in the shade, along with the other horses who had come to contest the Hanging Rock Cup. But this year was the first time Edward had a horse of his own to enter. The horse was being ridden by a local jockey who had shown his prowess on many horses and had ridden for the Blayney family on other occasions. The jockey stood nearby, preparing for the race, checking his saddle and equipment. Edward cast his practiced eye over all the other horses preparing for the race. His horse had at least as good breeding as any other horse running in the cup that day. He tried to remain calm, but his heart was racing as he brushed the already shiny coat of the giant stallion. The powerful smell of manure that filled the air barely registered with Edward. This just might be his chance to lift the Cup at the end of the race. He stroked the stallion's nose and whispered gently to him, spelling out his dreams and telling the horse that he knew he could win. The horse knew his master well and snuffled gently against Edward's shoulder.

The time of the race drew near. Edward had some last words of encouragement for the young jockey and moved towards the track to get a good view of the finishing post.

The horses were paraded around the mounting yard and then the jockeys mounted and galloped out onto the track. Edward's chest swelled with pride.

His father sidled up to him. Edward was proud of his father but as usual, he was a little worried that the Clerk of the Course would drink too much and make a scene. He wanted this day to be perfect.

"Good Luck, Edward," said Robert.

"Thank you, Father," he replied. "I reckon today is the day. Have you put a quid on him?"

"I have had a small wager, son," his father replied with a grin. With that, Robert hurried off to perform his duties.

Edward found his mother and stood close by her as the horses assembled at the starting line.

"Are you nervous, Edward?" whispered Charlotte.

"Yes, mother, incredibly so, but I know he can win."

"Well, good luck. They are about to go."

At that moment, the horses jumped, and the race began. Edward's horse did not start well and his heart sank. As they rounded the first bend, the horse was trailing the field. But Edward knew that if he could find some clear ground, he had a good burst of speed. The jockey pulled the horse to the outside and suddenly the horse exploded and seemed to double its speed. It moved to the outside on the widest part of the track and thundered down the straight, leaving all the other horses in its wake to win the race by a length.

Edward jumped for joy and hugged his mother. She laughed but held onto her hat as she attempted to maintain the dignity required of the wife of the Clerk of the Course.

Edward raced off to the winner's circle to greet his triumphant horse and jockey. He stroked the horse's nose. "I knew you could do it, my beauty!" he exclaimed. The young jockey was very pleased with himself and accepted Edward's congratulatory handshake and hearty pat on the back.

His father and the other racing officials presided over the presentation. As Edward held the cup over his head, he felt he would burst with pride. Soon he was surrounded by a bevy of young ladies who all wanted to congratulate him.

1888 Hesket

Charlotte watched the presentation with great pride in her handsome son. Edward was now 26 years old, with dark hair and a debonair moustache. But she could not hide her concern as all the young ladies gathered around him. Her son was a ladies' man, and she knew that his philandering could easily lead to a loss of the family reputation that she had fought so hard to maintain. It was true enough that rumours of Robert's run in with the law back in Wales abounded in the community. But to date, they had managed to keep the gossip at bay. Whilst the locals might suspect that the Blayneys had a convict background, they had no proof. And Charlotte was determined that it would stay that way.

Robert had mellowed somewhat over the last few years and had fewer confrontations and public scenes. But the same could not, unfortunately, be said for other members of the family. There had been quite a few days in court. But at least her brood were behaving reasonably well. Except that was for Edward.

She could not afford to allow Edward to bring all her hard work undone. His philandering had to be addressed. She needed to plant the seed of an idea to get him married off. She knew it would not be easy, as Edward had shown absolutely no interest in settling down.

That evening, as Robert and Charlotte lay in bed, Charlotte broached the subject.

"Robert, I am concerned about Edward. You must be well aware that he is quite the ladies' man."

"Oh well, yes, of course I am Charlotte. But he is young. He is just sowing his wild oats, as young men do."

"That is not a good attitude, Robert. If he keeps behaving like this, his name will be mud. It is not as if he is a teenager. He is a grown man with responsibilities. He must maintain the family dignity. You know how hard we have both worked to build our reputation as a community-minded family. And Michael's drinking and carousing has not helped. The last thing we need is for Edward to get some young woman into trouble. We need to get him married and to someone of his own station, not one of the servant girls he has been consorting with."

Robert looked at his wife, surprised at her suggestion.

"Oh really? And who would you suggest he marry, Charlotte?"

"Well, I don't really know, but what about Matilda, George and Susannah's daughter?"

"What? Do you really think he should marry his first cousin?"

"He has an affection for her. And she is getting on in years. She might jump at the chance to have a husband."

Robert could see that Charlotte had given the idea considerable thought, so he agreed to give it a try. They sat Edward down and broached the subject with him.

"Edward, we are rather worried about you. We think it is time you found a wife," said Charlotte. "Your brother has been married for several years now and you can see that he is very happy."

"I am not my brother," retorted Edward.

"I know that, but you are not exactly behaving in a manner that a young man should. We know that you have been seeing quite a few young ladies and mostly poor servant girls. It's not that these girls are not good enough. But surely it would be better if you courted someone who is more closely aligned to your present circumstances."

"Yes, Edward," said his father. "I understand that a young man should be allowed to sow his wild oats, however, it is important that you settle down soon."

"Robert, I don't think you should be encouraging him to 'sow his wild oats', as you so crudely put it. This is exactly the problem. Please be sensible." Frowning at Robert, she continued.

"We know you are very fond of your cousin, Matilda. Would she not make an appropriate match?"

"What? You must be joking. Why would I marry my first cousin?" he exclaimed.

"Well, it would give you some respectability for a start and Matilda is getting on in age. She may be delighted to consider an offer of marriage."

"That is out of the question. I don't want to marry anyone, let alone my cousin," replied Edward, and stormed out of the house.

Charlotte rose to follow him.

"Leave him," said Robert. "Give him some time to calm down and think about it. He is easily led and so might come around to your plan. But if we push him, that will be it. He will just get his back up and never agree."

Robert knew his son well and both Charlotte and Robert were soon watching on as Edward courted his cousin. It seemed she was happy to accept him as a suitor. Charlotte had spoken to Susannah, who at first had been outraged.

"What are you thinking, Charlotte?" said Susannah. "What on earth makes you think it would be a good idea for Edward to marry Matilda? She is his first cousin."

"Of course, I know that, and it is not what either of us would probably have wanted for our children. But Matilda is getting on in age and I am sure she would dearly love the respectability of marriage."

"Yes, well, I do have to agree with that. She is beginning to think she will be a spinster for the rest of her days."

"I see them together and they obviously have a great deal of affection for each other, so what could be the harm?"

"Yes, that is true. Perhaps we should just see where the friendship leads."

Susannah was still not completely convinced it was a good idea, but she knew her daughter craved a marriage. She discussed the proposal with George, and they both agreed that if it were to eventuate, they would not stand in Matilda's way.

Left to his own devices, Edward eventually asked Matilda to marry him and she accepted. The wedding was arranged.

Edward soon began to understand the benefits of having a wife who did not overly care what he did. And the gossips could hardly talk about his philandering now that he was a married man. He felt he had some small protection in order to resume his flirtations.

1890 Hesket

Charles and Jane were in Hesket again to check on the farm and see the family. Robert had mentioned that he was worried about Rebecca, so the brothers decided to pay her a visit.

"Perhaps you would like to pay a visit to Charlotte whilst we check on Rebecca, Jane?" Charles said.

"That sounds like an excellent idea," replied Jane. "It is some time since I have had a cup of tea with Charlotte."

The brothers left Jane to prepare to visit Charlotte and walked the short distance to Michael's farm. They ventured past Michael's home to the cottage where Rebecca was now living on her own. Rebecca appeared in answer to their knock. She looked slightly disheveled, but seemed well enough.

"How are you, Rebecca?" asked Charles giving his sister a hug. "It is lovely to see you."

"Oh really," said Rebecca. "I wonder how pleased you are to see me when you haven't visited for months."

"Now, Rebecca, you know that is not true. I visited last month when I was here to check up on my farm," answered Charles.

Rebecca looked confused. The two brothers could see that she couldn't remember the recent visits, and that concerned them. She was the firstborn of the family and was getting on in age, approaching 78 years. Charles, who was next born, was six years her junior and she was fourteen years older than her youngest brother Robert.

"What about a cup of tea, Rebecca?" suggested Robert, keen to spend some time with his older sister. She had become rather distant with him of late.

Rebecca went to the fire and busied herself with the kettle, making them tea. She put a handful of leaves in the teapot and poured in the water. Then she turned the teapot three times to the left and three times to the right. Charles and Robert smiled at this habit that they knew Rebecca had learned from their mother. Soon there were three steaming cups of tea on the table, together with a jug of milk and the sugar bowl.

"How have you been, Rebecca?" asked Charles as she sat down with them to drink her tea.

"I am well enough. The boys have been looking after me."

"Which boys?" asked Charles.

"Arthur and Henry."

Charles and Robert exchanged worried looks. They both considered Michael's two sons to be wild young men and wondered why they would be charged with looking after Rebecca. This was the first they had heard about any help being provided by Michael's sons, and neither Charles nor Robert could see how they would be any help to an elderly woman.

Charles was worried that he was not living up to the promise he made to his mother to look after Rebecca. He was not happy that she was living alone here with little support. He had tried over the years to convince her to come to live in Melbourne so that he could be closer to her. He felt it would be much better for her to distance herself from Michael and Agnes as their enmity had continued. But no matter how hard he tried, she would never agree to his proposal and now here she was supposedly being cared for by Michael's sons. The burden of guilt for the situation she was now in weighed heavily on Charles.

After finishing up their tea, the brothers took their leave, knowing that they needed to talk to Michael about the situation with Rebecca. They found him in the home paddock at the back of the cottage, rounding up some sheep.

"Michael, we are worried about Rebecca," said Charles.

"What about her?" asked Michael. "She has a perfectly good house to live in. She is fine."

"I think her health has deteriorated somewhat since Mother died. She doesn't really have a purpose anymore. I think it is telling in her behaviour."

"Well, you have nothing to worry about. The boys, Arthur and Henry, are looking after her."

"So she said," replied Robert. "But what possible help can they be to an old lady? They don't know how to look after themselves and keep out of trouble. They would be better doing some of the work on the farm. It is in a bad enough state."

Michael frowned and spots of colour rose in his cheeks.

"What do you mean? My boys are fine and they are helping her. They do their share of work on the farm. You two need to mind your own business. And as for you, Charles, you are only here when it suits you."

"Alright Michael, I understand that you have been here more than me," said Charles. "What Robert means is that Rebecca is getting older and may need some more help."

Agnes appeared at the back door of the house. It seemed she had been listening to the conversation.

"She is definitely losing her mind," she said. "She comes in here and tries to tell me how to run my life and look after my family. As if she would know anything about running a family, being a barren old spinster. She has no idea. She can't even remember what day it is."

"That is exactly my point, Agnes," replied Charles calmly. "She needs her family to look after her. And I am just not sure if the boys are the best candidates for the job."

"And what would you know? You swan in here when it suits you and try to tell us what to do. You think you are some sort of a special gentleman with all your airs and graces. But I know where you came from. You were just as dirt poor as your brothers when you came here."

Charles and Robert could see they were not going to get any sense from the couple, so they took their leave.

"This is a significant problem, Charles," said Robert.

"I agree," said Charles. "We will need to keep a close eye on the boys."

1891 Hesket

Matilda was in the garden watering the vegetable patch when she saw someone walking through the wheat crop.

"Edward," she called, "there is someone walking through the crop. Won't that damage it?"

Edward was inside dressing.

"Who is it?" he called.

"I can't tell," She replied.

Edward came out into the yard and as the interloper drew nearer, he could see that it was his father's brother, Michael.

"What are you doing walking through my crop? Get out of there."

"I am looking for a stray turkey. My daughter Ada said it was in your crop but that you wouldn't let her get it."

"Well, I haven't seen any turkey, you old fool."

"That is no way to talk to an old man." Michael and his boys, Arthur and Henry, had been grubbing potatoes all day. It had been a long, hot day. Michael was spoiling for a fight.

"Come on, stand up to me like a man?"

"No, I do not want to fight you."

With that, Michael threw a punch at the younger man, who tried to block the punch. It surprised Edward how quickly the situation had escalated. But then again, he knew Michael was easily angered.

Arthur and Henry had been watching this scene transpire and when they saw their father and Edward start fighting, they jumped the fence and ran to their father's aid.

"Leave the old man alone," cried Arthur, "have a go at me."

He shaped up to Edward, leaving him no choice other than to defend himself and the two young men set to, both throwing punches, very few of them actually connecting. Matilda picked up a stick that was lying nearby and tried to separate the two men, raining blows on both of them. One blow landed heavily on Edward, knocking him to the ground. Henry grabbed the stick to disarm Matilda and she was knocked down, banging her head against the log fence.

Arthur went to kick Edward as he lay on the ground. But his father pulled him away.

"Leave him, he has had enough," he said.

The three men walked away, leaving Edward to help Matilda to her feet.

Edward overheard the conversation as the men walked away.

"Why didn't you let me finish him off?" Arthur asked his father.

"Don't be a fool. You know what they are like. No doubt we will end up in court after today. Do you want a serious assault charge?"

Matilda and Edward were both sporting injuries, so they made their way to Woodend to see the Doctor. Edward was treated for a cut on his face, a broken nose and bruises on his face and hands. Matilda had lost a tooth and had a cut and bruising on her head.

After they had been treated for their injuries, they reported the incident to the local sergeant.

Sergeant Tucker sighed as he listened to their story. He was well used to the bickering that went on in the Blayney family.

"Do you want to press charges?" he asked wearily.

"Of course, we want to press charges," replied Edward. "This was a serious assault."

And so, the next week found them all in the Woodend Court. Robert and his son sat in the court together with Matilda. There were nine charges in all, once Michael and his sons had countered Edward's charges. The judge decided to hear all charges at once as they all related to the same matter.

Arthur was the first to give his evidence.

"I was in our yard and watched as Father went across the log fence and was confronted by Edward. Edward punched Father and grabbed him by the coat. I ran over the fence to help Father. I said to Edward, 'Why are you hitting an old man?' He didn't reply except to aim a fist at my face. I dodged and said, 'If that's the way you want to settle it, let's go'. Then we started fighting. My brother Henry had followed me over.

"Matilda had picked up a stick and started hitting me. But she hit Edward too and knocked him to the ground. That was when Henry grabbed the stick and, in the process of trying to take it from her so she could do no further damage, she fell to the ground and knocked her head on the fence. Father told us to come away and leave them alone, so we left and went back to our yard."

The judge then called Michael to give his evidence.

"I walked across the paddock looking for the turkey. Edward called out, 'What are you doing in there, you old bastard'. I told him I was looking for the turkey and that walking in the crop would not do any harm. I asked him why he would talk to an old man like that. He didn't answer me, but hit me instead. Then Arthur appeared and Edward shaped up to him."

"Did he shape up well?" asked the Judge slightly amused at the evidence being given.

"I thought his wife shaped up better," replied Michael with a grin.

"But she ended up on the ground. Henry was trying to separate Edward and Arthur. And he would have been able to if Matilda had not been waving her stick around. That is why Henry dragged the stick away from her."

Henry corroborated the evidence given by his father and brother and added that he had not pushed Matilda, but had merely tried to remove the stick from her.

Now it was Edward's turn to tell his side of the story.

"After Matilda told me that someone was walking through our crop, I came out to see who it was. I saw that it was Michael Blayney, and I asked him why he was there. He said that he was looking for a turkey. I told him I did not believe that because I had not seen any turkeys in the crop. He asked if I wanted to fight and I said no. But he came towards me in a threatening manner. I thought he was going to hit me and put my arms up to protect myself. Then Arthur turned up and started hitting me. I tried to defend myself but got knocked to the ground. Then he kicked me. I saw Henry push Matilda and knock her to the ground. Fortunately, that was when they decided that they had done enough damage and left. I helped Matilda up, and we both made our way to the Doctor."

The final witness was the Doctor who gave evidence that Matilda and Edward had been treated at his surgery and described their injuries.

The Judge then retired and returned after about 20 minutes of deliberation, to deliver his verdict.

"I find the charges brought by Michael, Arthur, and Henry Blayney are not substantiated and are therefore dismissed. I order payment of £1 costs for these charges. Further, I find the charges of assault bought by Edward and Matilda Blayney to be proven, and fine each of the defendants 40 shillings. You have 24 hours to pay the fines or go to jail for 7 days."

Michael, Arthur, and Henry rose and shouted at the judge as their solicitor tried to caution them.

The judge retired and Robert, Edward and Matilda left the courtroom quickly, without a glance at their relatives so as not to inflame the situation further. But they were very pleased with the result. They were sick of Michael and his bully sons. They deserved to be put in their place.

Chapter Fifteen

1892 Newham

John and Elizabeth sat by the fire in their large comfortable home. Outside the sun was setting on a dreary winter day. John looked fondly at his wife who despite her advancing years still looked to John like the young girl he had married all those years ago. They were both now in their sixties and still very much in love. Elizabeth had given John twelve children, the oldest now 32 whilst the youngest was 9. They were a large boisterous but very happy family. All of their children had been baptised in the Baptist faith and the entire family still attended services together.

But John was feeling a deep sadness. Today they had buried his beloved mother. The entire extended family had gathered at the graveside together with a large number of members of their church and community. John knew his family was well respected and the attendance at the funeral bore this out.

It was only 12 months since they had buried his father in the same cemetery plot. Samuel had lived to the grand old age of 83 years and John was proud of all his father had achieved in his long and successful life. He was also proud of the part he had been able to play in that life. But he missed his father dreadfully.

He felt sure that his mother had actually died of grief. She had been inconsolable and had deteriorated quickly. After all, she was also an old woman. She was 84 years of age when she died.

John was jolted out of his reverie by a knock on the door. After the wake everyone had departed and John was a little disappointed to have his peace disturbed this late in the day.

He answered the door and found Harold and Grace standing there. He breathed a sigh of relief. If there was anyone he could talk to on a night such as this it was his beloved sister Grace and of course Harold was one of his oldest friends.

"How are you Grace?" he asked his sister, knowing that her grief would be a raw as his own.

"I am alright thank you," she replied. "It has been a long and sad day. I will miss them both dreadfully."

Elizabeth had risen from her seat by the fire and was soon pouring tea for them all from the large teapot. The kettle was always on the boil on these cold winter nights.

As they sat sipping tea, the conversation turned invariably to the never-ending conflict over the Hanging Rock Reserve. John knew that Harold was trying to distract them from their grief but he wasn't sure he felt like entering into this discussion tonight of all nights.

"Have you heard that the Victorian Racing Commission are demanding that the track be extended? It seems that they will not allow racing to continue unless the track is upgraded."

"No I hadn't heard that," replied John, his interest piqued despite himself. "Perhaps this is our chance to have racing stopped in our reserve. After all there are racecourses nearby at Woodend. There really is no need to continue racing here at Hanging Rock."

"We would have quite a fight on our hands again to try to prevent the upgrades," said Harold. "The Blayney family for one would certainly put up a fight."

"Yes, well things are going from bad to worse with that family. Did you read about their latest court appearance in the paper?"

"I most certainly did. I find it rather unbelievable that any family would actually throw punches at each other."

Chapter Sixteen

1895 Hesket

Charlotte sat in her kitchen, taking a moment to relax and look at the Foy and Gibson catalogue Jane had sent from Melbourne. She was feeling pleased with herself as she had finally been able to convince Robert to spend some money on their home. They agreed that Charlotte should have some cash for housekeeping. Now she had some of the comforts she had longed for. There was glass in the windows and bright coloured curtains hung over the glass. They had installed a shiny new wood stove in the corner of the kitchen. She no longer needed to feel inadequate when she entertained in her home. A beautiful tea set and silverware graced her table when she served tea to guests.

They even had servants' quarters now. She had employed Martha Soames to help around the house. Martha was only 14 years old, but she was mature for her age. She reminded Charlotte of herself at a similar age. After her parents had died, when Charlotte was not much older than Martha, she had no choice but to go into service. She grew up quickly as she navigated the difficult hierarchy of an English manor house. Charlotte was aware that Martha was also in a dubious situation at her home. Martha's father, Alex Soames, was a strong disciplinarian and had been very strict with her upbringing. Martha's mother had never been able to stand up to her husband where Martha was concerned. Although Alex had never physically abused his wife, she was fearful of him and tried never to do anything to displease him.

When Martha first arrived at the Blayney household, she was extremely timid. However, she blossomed into a happy and charming young girl, nurtured by Charlotte's kindly nature. Charlotte knew that Martha had been glad to leave the family home to work for them, even if it was as a lowly servant.

At that moment Martha entered the kitchen, her arms laden with freshly washed clothing.

"What a perfect day for drying the washing, Mrs Blayney," she said brightly. "Just enough wind so that it has dried perfectly but not got wrapped around the line."

"That's good Martha." replied Charlotte. "Now get it folded and put away, please. The iron is heating on the stove if anything needs ironing."

Martha hummed happily as she went about the task. Charlotte smiled as she watched Martha. They got along very well. It was a pleasure to have her around.

1897 Hesket

The plants in the Blayney's garden brought a bright splash of colour to the otherwise muted landscape. Charlotte loved her garden. For years, she had focused on growing vegetables to feed the family. She grew cabbages, peas, beans and spinach in neat rows. Pumpkin vines ranged over a large garden bed. Vines also grew over the walls of the cottage. Now that her children were growing, she could spend more time tending her precious exotic plants. There were roses, oleanders and magnolias and a range of annuals from which she collected the seeds to regrow each year. Besides these she also had banksias, wattles and other native shrubs. Charlotte had planted cyprus and birch trees quite early on and they were now reaching a good height. The gums that surrounded the cottage were also welcome in her garden landscape. They appeared to only contain muted green and grey at first glance. But Charlotte appreciated the multitude of colours that made up their trunks. From radiant white to pitch black and so much in between. Some featured bare trunks and branches where the wind had whipped off all the peeling bark, trunks of so many colours, pale green, white, salmon pink, cream, but all smooth and graceful. Then there were those with harsh, black cracked bark. The evergreen leaves were mostly a dark green with some blue grey, but in spring the shiny new growth ranged from bright green to iridescent red. The gums also had many extraordinary flowers in red, orange and yellow.

This pleasing scene greeted Martha as she wandered through the garden. She had an eye for pretty things. The plant in the corner of the garden caught her attention. As a whole it looked astonishingly beautiful, with its multitude of colourful flowers, but as she looked closer she could see the individual beauty of each single flower. Five perfectly shaped purple petals surrounded the bright red centre, which reached out into the petals with sharp tendrils of colour. From the centre of this beauty emerged the stamen, bright neutral white against the colour of the flower. Tiny pieces of pollen scattered gently on the petals. She leant in to smell the delicate fragrance.

Martha stepped on a piece of bark that last night's stormy wind had stripped from the gum trees. It produced a satisfying crunch. Her mind wandered as she moved on through the garden on her way to the vegetable patch. She loved the chance to spend time in the garden, so she was always happy to volunteer to collect the vegetables for the evening meal.

She thought about many things, but suddenly her mind moved to him. *What was it about him? Why was she so taken in by him?* She knew she could never realise her desire for him because she was a mere servant and he was the master's son. She must stop this. No good would come of her daydreams.

And then suddenly he was there. Edward, the young and handsome eldest son of the family, appeared on the garden path in front of her. He smiled his roguish smile, and she blushed. Martha was well aware of Edward's philandering ways. She could not work in the household without hearing the gossip surrounding his many affairs. His family had convinced him to take his first cousin for his wife to try to still the tongues of the local gossips. Martha suspected it was a loveless marriage of convenience for both of them. She could understand why Matilda had agreed to marry Edward as she was passing the age when young women were expected to marry. Despite everything that warned her against it, Martha could not help but be attracted to him.

"Good morning, Martha," he said. She could tell that he knew how his greeting affected her.

"Good morning, sir," she replied, casting her eyes to the ground but wanting to listen to his voice forever.

"Come sit with me for a moment," he said, indicating the wrought iron garden bench.

"Oh no sir, I couldn't possibly. I must get back to my work."

She made to move past him to continue to the vegetable garden. But he blocked her path.

"Come, there is nothing to be afraid of. Can't you spare me just a few moments?"

"Well, maybe just a moment," she said, thinking that this was the only way she would be able to convince him to let her continue. They moved to the bench, and she sat stiffly on the edge of the seat. She was nervous that they would be discovered, but could not control her delight that he seemed to want to be in her company.

"The garden is impressive at the moment, isn't it?" he said. "Those flowers that you admired are stunning."

"Oh yes," she agreed, "they really are so beautiful and the bushes are covered in blooms." She realised how quickly and easily he had been able to draw her into the conversation, a thought that disturbed her somewhat. She was also aware that he must have been watching her.

He stood up and wandered over to a nearby bush and plucked one of the flowers. Wandering back and sitting back down, he offered the colourful bloom to her.

"It is nearly as beautiful as you," he said.

She blushed deep red and jumped up from the seat. "I really must get on," she stammered and picking up her basket, she hurried on to get her vegetables.

When she arrived at the vegetable garden and turned to survey the seat from a safe distance to ensure he had left, she was breathless and agitated. She had certainly not expected him to say such a thing. But although she felt troubled by her feelings, she felt a warm glow in her body as she allowed herself to think about what he had said and to imagine a life where she could spend time with him.

She shook herself. She must not think like that. They could never be more than master and servant. She was very fortunate to have obtained this position in Robert Blayney's household. He was a bit eccentric and drank too much, but he was generally well respected in the community. There were rumours about his background, some said he had come to the colony as a convict, but he had amassed a great deal of wealth. She held a prime position in his household and she must not do anything to jeopardise it.

But as time passed, she saw more and more of Edward. He continued to pay her compliments, and soon her head was turned. She became more relaxed in his presence as he convinced her that nobody would mind.

One evening, as she was heading to her bedroom at the end of a long day, she bumped into him. She knew he had no business being in the servants' quarters, which meant he had come looking for her. He leaned in close to her and whispered in her ear. "You are so beautiful. Will you let me kiss you?"

"Oh, please, I can't," she replied breathlessly.

"Oh, but you can, you know," he said.

His breath in her ear made her feel faint, and a warm feeling spread through her body.

He touched his mouth to her lips and kissed her gently. She returned the kiss for just a second and then pulled away.

"I am sorry," she said and hurried past him to her bedroom. She locked the door and stood with her back against it, breathing heavily.

No matter how hard she tried she could not resist him and soon the tryst between the two lovers blossomed until one day Martha sought Edward out in the paddock where he was tending the sheep. She was tearful and struggled to find the words to tell Edward about the predicament she found herself in.

"What is it, Martha?" he asked. He smiled sympathetically at her. Martha was sure that his feelings for her were real.

"Edward, I am with child," she was eventually able to stutter through her tears.

Edward looked stunned and for a moment, could not find any words.

"What, you can't be. Surely not!" he finally managed to blurt out.

"There is little doubt. It will be obvious soon."

They kept their dreadful secret for some weeks until Martha began to show. Charlotte guessed the girl's predicament. Although Martha was terrified of Edward's father, she had developed a friendship with the sensible Charlotte. She looked to Charlotte as a motherly figure, even though she was the mistress of the house.

Through her tears, Martha confessed.

"Yes, I am with child. Whatever will I do?"

"Who is the father?" asked Charlotte.

Martha looked alarmed. "I can't possibly tell you that," she whispered, although she knew Charlotte had probably guessed.

"Well, if you are not willing to tell me, you will need to leave our employ and return to your father's house. You cannot expect us to continue to support you if you are going to keep your secret."

Martha gasped. "Oh no, please, I can't go back. My father will never accept my baby."

"Well, you must tell me," said Charlotte.

"But please, I can't."

ele

Charlotte decided to take the matter up with her son. She sought him out, away from prying ears at the house.

"Edward, Martha has just told me she is with child." It was a bland statement, but Edward knew that his mother could see right through him. He wondered if there was any point in trying to hide the facts from his mother. He decided there was not.

"The child could be mine," he said miserably.

"What do you mean could be?" his mother asked. "Are you accusing the girl of having more than one beau?"

"Oh no, of course not, she loves me." The words were out of Edward's mouth before he could stop himself.

This did not, however, surprise Charlotte. She knew her son well enough to know that he was indeed in love with the lovely young Martha.

"So, this child is yours?"

"It must be so," came the strangled response.

"And what do you propose to do about it?"

"I don't know."

"Well, you are going to have to tell your father for a start and we will need to placate him if you don't want Martha to have to return to her family home."

"You know she can't do that. We must convince father to allow her to stay."

That evening, when Robert came in from a hard day of work on the farm, Charlotte cleared the room of the other members of her family.

"Edward has something to tell you," she said.

Robert looked up from his glass. He was still in the habit of partaking in just one or two drinks before dinner after a hard day.

"Well?" he looked at Edward.

Edward could not look at his father. He stood with his eyes downcast, but could not find the words.

"Speak up Edward," said his father impatiently.

"Martha is with child and Edward is responsible," said Charlotte, taking pity on her son.

"What?" blustered Robert, jumping to his feet.

"Yes, there is no doubt," replied Charlotte.

"Is this true?" asked Robert.

Edward recoiled in the face of his father's anger. He could still not seem to find any words and simply nodded his head.

"Well, what do you propose to do about the situation? You are a married man."

"Yes, Father but you know as well as I do that I have no love for my wife. And there is very little likelihood that she will ever present me with a son."

Despite his displeasure at the situation, Robert took pity on his son, and Martha was allowed to stay. Charlotte was rather relieved because she had no wish to send the girl back to her father. Martha continued her duties in the kitchen, right up to the time of the birth. Her son was born in the early hours of a hot January morning.

Edward tried hard to hide his pride. Martha and the baby remained on the farm. Edward wondered whether his wife suspected. He thought it most likely that she knew well enough that he was the father.

There were, of course, rumours around the district. But they didn't amount to anything, especially when Robert and Charlotte had allowed Martha to remain as a servant in their home. Consequently, Edward was able to enjoy a relationship, of sorts, with his son.

Rebecca's health had deteriorated further in the last few years. Now in her 83rd year she was suffering from senility and didn't really even know her family. Charles and Robert tried to guide her, but unfortunately, they feared that her nephews, Arthur and Henry, had taken advantage of her. They had moved into the small home with Rebecca and now she was basically under lock and key. The rest of the family felt sure that the boys were attempting to get her to sign the house and the small amount of money her parents had left her over to them. Robert and Charles knew that Rebecca would have been horrified had she been in her right mind. She had previously had no time for the two boys or any of Michael and Agnes's children. But in her current state, she did not know that they were taking advantage of her.

Her brothers were, of course, alarmed at the situation. Something had to be done. On his next visit to his property in West Melbourne, Robert, with Charlotte, paid a visit to Charles and Jane. The women chatted happily and enjoyed a glass of sherry. The two brothers sat with the crystal brandy decanter between them and savoured their evening tipple as they discussed the problem they faced.

"We shall have to do something about those young scoundrels," said Charles.

"Yes, but what?" asked Robert. "Rebecca thinks they are looking after her. I know you have tried to convince her to move to Melbourne but we are unlikely to get her to leave the home she has lived in for so long. The only answer is to move those boys out. I don't think Rebecca has signed anything over to them yet. But how would we know? You must come back to Hesket with me to sort it out."

"Very well," said Charles. "Although I really don't know what we will be able to do. I am sure we won't get any help from Michael and Agnes."

They prepared for the journey to their country homes. Arriving late in the evening, they decided to delay their task until the following morning.

The next day, Robert was on Charles's doorstep before Charles and Jane had time to fully prepare for the day. But Charles knew he had to try to talk some sense into Michael's sons, so he may as well get it over with. For one thing, they had heard that Rebecca was not well and they needed to get her to see a doctor.

"Now Robert, you will need to remain calm," said Charles. "Losing your temper is not going to help."

Unfortunately, Robert had already worked himself up into quite a state.

"I will do what needs to be done," replied Robert. "They can't possibly think that they can just take control of Rebecca, particularly if she is not well enough to look after herself."

The two brothers made the short walk to their sister's cottage. It was immediately obvious that the cottage had been let go. Up until recently, Rebecca had kept up her mother's garden and had always taken good care of her chickens and turkeys. But now the garden was overgrown, and the chickens ranged around the yard. Loose shingles flapped on the roof of the cottage.

Charles and Robert looked at each other as they approached. They had let their sister down by not checking up on her sooner. Each man wondered if the other felt similarly guilty over their failure to take care of Rebecca as they had promised their mother.

Arthur met them at the gate. He was an angry young man and was well known to be a heavy drinker like his father. His hair was unkempt and his clothing was dirty and ragged.

"Hello Arthur," said Charles calmly.

"What are you doing here?" asked Henry, appearing from the side of the cottage, and looking every bit as rough and unkempt as his brother.

"We have just come to see our sister. We are worried that she is not well. Has she seen a doctor yet?"

"That's none of your business."

"It most certainly is our business," said Robert.

"Now calm down, Robert," said Charles, knowing that this would not end well if he couldn't keep his brother under control.

"Arthur, we are coming in to see Rebecca," said Robert.

"No, you are not," said Arthur.

Robert had had enough by this point.

"We'll see about that," he shouted. And before Charles had a chance to intervene, Robert had attempted to open the gate. Arthur was determined that Robert would not get in. He picked up the axe from the wood heap and charged towards the gate. He swung the axe at Robert, by this time too enraged to control himself. The axe caught Robert over both forearms. Robert screamed in agony.

The scream brought Rebecca from the house.

"What is going on?" she asked, obviously distressed. She did not understand what had caused Robert to scream at the top of his lungs.

Charles tried to calm the situation.

"It's alright Rebecca, don't worry. Go back inside. I will take care of Robert. I will take him home and then come back to see you. You boys had better let me in when I get back." He threw a threatening glance at the young brothers. By now, both Arthur and Henry knew they were in serious trouble. Arthur had gone deathly pale and sat on a stump with his head in his hands.

Charles knew Robert was in a bad way, so he decided he had no choice but to leave now and return later to check on Rebecca.

He helped Robert to his feet, and they both left with Robert moaning in pain. Charles took him home to Charlotte, who was horrified once she heard the full story. They immediately sent to Woodend for the Doctor who diagnosed broken bones in both arms.

Charles knew they could not let this rest. After ensuring that Robert was taken care of, he rode to the Police Station in Woodend. The young constable accompanied him back to Rebecca's home. After hearing the full story and questioning both Arthur and Henry, the constable charged Arthur with assault.

"You cannot allow him to stay here. He has been menacing my sister, and I am afraid for her safety," said Charles.

At Charles's insistence, the young constable led Arthur away and he was taken to the lockup in Woodend.

"And you, Henry, leave this house at once. Go back to your father and mother and tell them what has happened. You are not to come back to Rebecca's home. Do you hear me?"

Charles' patience was by now wearing thin, and Henry was at least wise enough to know when to leave.

Meanwhile, Charles needed to get the Doctor to check on Rebecca who was still at the forefront of his mind. He hurried back to Robert's house and as soon as the Doctor had seen to Robert's injuries, they both hurried back to Rebecca's house.

Charles was anxious not to let any more time pass before his sister was attended to. Rebecca, however, was not particularly pleased to see them.

"Please, Rebecca, you must let us in. You need to see the Doctor."

"What are you doing?" she asked when the doctor attempted to examine her.

"You are not well Rebecca, the Doctor needs to check you out."

"There's nothing wrong with me," she said, but finally she allowed the doctor to check her over and swallowed the tonic he prescribed.

Once again, the Blayney family found themselves in court. But given the seriousness of the situation on this occasion, they were all subdued. Rebecca was not in a fit state to give evidence, but both Robert and Charles presented the facts. This was a serious assault. Robert had both arms splinted and bandaged. Arthur was found guilty of assault and the Judge sentenced him to six months in jail. He would serve his time in Pentridge with hard labour. This did nothing to improve the relations in the Blayney family.

Meanwhile, Robert's condition deteriorated. The broken bones were not healing well. And he was not one to sit around and do nothing, so this exacerbated the problem. He could not ride his beloved horses and grew more morose and angrier by the day.

Edward tried to be there for his father. He sat with him and talked of the horses and how well they were doing. The breeding was improving with each new foal. Robert sat quietly and listened, but his temperament did not improve.

1898 Hesket

Charlotte had not been feeling well for many months now. She felt shaky and had a lot less energy than in her younger days. She had prided herself in keeping an immaculate house and had been so proud of her garden. Now, much to her displeasure, she did not seem to have the energy to keep the large beds under control. If she was honest, she had probably started feeling unwell years ago. She tried very hard to hide her malady from her family, but over the last year or so, her children often enquired if she was alright.

Now, at 72 years of age, she was no longer a young woman. Maybe she was coming to the end of her time. She thought back over the last few years. She had convinced Robert to afford them some luxuries, and they now lived comfortably in both their country and city homes. But Robert seemed destroyed. He had still not fully recovered from the injuries at the hands of his wicked nephew, Arthur. He was morose and difficult to live with. No matter how much she and the rest of the family tried, they could not bring him out of his black mood. He had been so withdrawn that Charlotte did not think he had even noticed that she was unwell. She knew she had no option but to see a doctor. She asked Edward and Matilda to take her to Woodend.

"Hello Charlotte, how are you?" asked the Doctor. "I have noticed you have not been looking well of late." They had come to know each other well over the many months he had been caring for Robert.

"Yes, I have been very shaky and extremely tired and don't seem to have any strength. All my chores are getting harder."

"Do you have any pain?" he asked.

"Sometimes but not bad."

"Well, I will prescribe a tonic and laudanum for the pain. But I think you will need to get plenty of bed rest. It could be a disease that is being referred to as shaky palsy."

They went out to where Edward and Matilda were waiting.

"Hello Edward, hello Matilda," said the Doctor. "Your Mother needs bed rest. You and the family will need to look after her."

Despite everyone's best efforts to take care of her, it was not long before Charlotte was confined to her bed. Even Robert tried to rouse himself from his lethargy to assist with Charlotte's care. But it was all to no avail.

Gradually she sank further and further until her illness consumed her and she passed away in her sleep on March 16, 1898.

Chapter Seventeen

1900 Hesket

Robert was devastated by Charlotte's death and soon sank back into his previous state of depression and anger. He missed her dreadfully and often felt angry that she had left him alone. Now he had to deal with his wayward son without her help.

He regretted letting Charlotte talk him into allowing Martha to stay in their household. He knew his son well and had foreseen that he would not stay away from Martha. And now he had been proven right. Martha was again with child.

It had not been a happy relationship between Edward and his wife; he knew that. And he wondered at that decision too, to force Edward to marry. Once again, Charlotte's idea. However, there was nothing he could do about that now. He had to deal with the current situation.

"This is a disaster, Martha. You cannot remain in this house if this is how you treat our trust."

"But I can't go home, sir," Martha wept loudly.

"You have no choice. Go and pack your things."

Edward, to give him some credit, tried to intervene for Martha, even though he knew it would send his father into a greater rage.

He sought out his father where he sat outside under the verandah. It was a bright spring day and seedlings were starting to flourish in the rich black soil. The chickens pecked at the ground around the edges of the garden, the fence preventing them from scratching the new seedlings.

"Please, Father, you can't make her leave," pleaded Edward.

But Robert was having none of it.

"Edward, you cannot expect me to allow this woman to stay in our home. She has disgraced herself again, and you have taken advantage of her. She has a home to go to, and that is where she must go."

"But Father, surely you know how harsh her father is. He will not make it an easy life for Martha. I just hope he doesn't take it out on the children."

Edward knew that this would give his father pause. He was fond of his grandchildren, including Martha's handsome young son. But Edward could not sway him.

"No Edward, stop, you cannot change my mind. I should never have allowed Martha to stay in the first place. If she is away from you, she may have some hope of finding someone to marry, though I don't know how she will do that with two illegitimate children."

So Martha returned to her father's home. She packed up her things and, together with her son, she grudgingly walked the few miles to her father's home.

"What have you done?" asked her father as he saw her belongings. Martha was silent, her eyes downcast. "Out with it. What has happened? Why have you been turned away from a good position?"

"I am with child, Father," she whispered fearfully.

"What? Again?" her father exploded. "This can't be. Who is the father?"

"I can't tell you that," replied Martha. She knew it would only anger her father further should she tell him.

"If you won't tell me you can leave, I will not have you under my roof." Martha and her mother and son cowered under the anger of her father.

"Oh Father, please, I don't know what to do. I have nowhere else to go. My son needs a home."

"You honestly expect me to just let you walk back in here as if nothing has happened?"

Her father was a strict and sometimes cruel man but as his anger cooled slowly he realised he could not turn his daughter away. This boy, illegitimate or not, was his grandson. He turned to his wife, and she looked at him imploring but wordlessly.

Martha and her son would stay.

Robert sat under the verandah, drinking his morning cup of tea. His head throbbed from overindulgence with the bottle the previous evening. Now that he had little to occupy his time, because of his injured arms, he was glad of the comfort of his home. Despite himself, he was grateful that Charlotte had nagged him to spend his hard-earned money on these comforts. In the summer, the wide verandah was his favorite place to sit. A huge oak tree, seeds of which had been brought from Wales by the family, grew close by and provided shade on these hot days. He surveyed the garden that Charlotte had been so fond of and saw that it was in need of some care. It made him even sadder when he thought of how much he missed his beautiful wife. She was the best thing that had ever happened to him, and he knew he had not always made her life easy.

The only other pastime that stilled his temper somewhat and gave him some contentment was when he was able to get to Melbourne to see his brother Charles and spend time working in the city business. Whilst he had always preferred his farm life before his injuries, he now felt that at least he could be of some use there, seeing to the book-keeping.

He looked up from his reverie as the old gate creaked and saw that Alex Soames was walking up the pathway. *Here's trouble*, he thought.

"Robert, we need to talk," said Alex. "Your son must take responsibility for the trouble he has caused my Martha."

"Oh, and what trouble is that?" asked Robert, wondering how he could get Alex to leave before his temper got the better of him.

"You know very well what I am referring to. That young whelp has taken advantage of my daughter and now she has not one but two children to care for. He needs to provide for them."

"Is that so?" came the wry response from Robert. "What makes you so sure my son is the father of those children?"

"Oh, come on, you can't be serious. Of course, he is the father. Those two have been fraternising for years. He needs to look after the children. Anyway, I am only here to tell you I intend to take him to court. Where is he, by the way?"

"I am not sure, exactly. He left for Melbourne a month ago."

"Well, you had better let him know that I will see him in court." Alex turned on his heel and left the way he had come.

Robert frowned. He knew all too well that Edward had fathered the two children. Robert was very proud that the family business had been successful and had grown enough that he had been able to employ some servants and farmhands. But no one had foreseen the trouble it would cause the Blayney family.

Robert was sure that Edward still loved the young woman and that he had been providing financial assistance to help support Martha to look after the children for several years. He was angry and surprised that Alex would want to drag it all through the courts. But Edward was going to have to face the music.

Edward arrived back in Hesket in time for the court case.

He and his father sat and shared a drink on the verandah.

"Well, son, there is no getting away from it now. You have to deal with this problem. Do you propose to admit that the children are yours?"

Edward looked sheepish. This was not the sort of thing he and his father usually discussed.

"What should I do, Father? You know I love her. But can I admit that the children are mine? I need to present a professional image to further my business interests. And I also need to consider Matilda as well. She has been a good wife to me. She doesn't deserve this scandal."

Robert frowned. "I know what you mean son, it is important to keep up appearances. Perhaps you should make it clear that you will continue to provide financial support for the children but not confirm that you are their father."

"Yes, I think that will be the best course of action."

The day of the court case arrived.

Edward was asked whether he would support the children.

"I have always assisted Martha in the upbringing of these children. But I do not admit that they are mine." As he said this, he looked at Martha and saw the hurt in her eyes. He had not spoken to her for many months. They had both agreed that they needed to finish whatever it was that was between them. They both needed to go their separate ways and get on with their lives. That was what Edward had agreed to anyway. He was not so sure about Martha. He could understand her hurt and anger. She was an unmarried mother with two illegitimate children. The community treated her with disdain whilst Edward went about his business, bearing little consequence of his part in her situation. He was sure she felt the injustice of the situation sorely.

The judge asked Martha whether, in fact, she had received financial support for the children.

"Yes, except for a missed payment on the odd occasion," answered Martha, trying to maintain her dignity. It upset her that her father was dragging this all through the courts. "I have always had assistance from Edward. It was not my idea to be here today. I would prefer to leave things as they are."

"In that case, why are we wasting everyone's time?" said the judge impatiently. "Why is this matter before the courts? Case dismissed."

Martha left the court, closely followed by her father without a backward glance at Edward. He was saddened and ashamed. He knew it was wrong to disown the children. But what choice did he have? He quietly resolved that he would continue to provide for them. It was tragic that Martha was left on her own to deal with the children and her tyrannical father, but that would be an end to it.

Chapter Eighteen

1902 Hesket

The intervening years had been tough on Robert. Now his heart was simply giving out. He lay in his sickbed and murmured slowly. Edward and the rest of his family despaired. There appeared to be no way that they could lift him out of this melancholy that seemed to be sending him to his grave.

The murmurings stilled momentarily, and Robert's eyes opened. He saw his son was sitting by his bedside. Edward started as his father spoke.

"I can't believe it has all come to this," whispered Robert.

"What do you mean?" asked Edward. His father had been a fiery and erratic parent, but Edward loved and respected him.

"Our family has disintegrated," said Robert. "There has been so much angst. I am sure that poor Rebecca died as result of her ill treatment at the hands of Arthur and Henry. We should never have let them move into her house."

Rebecca had died the year before, reaching the grand old age of 89 years. Edward rather doubted that she had any memory at all of the attack on his father, let alone that it had led to her death.

"Michael and Agnes have let their farm run down. It's a disgrace. After all the hard work I did to ensure he had a place to come to once he had served his sentence. He does nothing to keep that wretched wife of his in line."

"Father, you should not worry about them. They have brought their problems on themselves," said Edward.

"And you, my boy, siring two illegitimate children, taking advantage of a young girl who knew no better. I really don't think I can take much more. It is all too much for a man my age. Life is just not worth living without my darling Charlotte."

Edward thought Robert was being rather melodramatic, but he continued to try to lift his father's spirits.

"Oh Father, please don't talk like that. You have plenty of good years left in you. You can't throw in the towel now. What will become of the horses? Charles and Jane will be here to see you tomorrow."

Edward knew that if anyone could talk his father out of this dark mood, it would be Charles. They had always been close.

Once again, Charles and Jane made the journey to Hesket to be there for Robert, but it was no use. He continued to deteriorate and before too long they laid him in his grave in the Woodend cemetery, in a plot not too distant from his mother and father and with his beloved wife Charlotte.

1902 Woodend

Not long after Robert's death, the dispute over the Hanging Rock Reserve again reared its head. Not that it had ever really died down. The Newham Shire Council and the Lands Department were in continual receipt of correspondence from one side or the other. Now the Minister for Lands, Mr. Albert Tucker, would be paying a visit to meet with the locals. John

Marlowe and his supporters were very keen to hear what the Minister had to say.

The meeting was to take place in Woodend. As the Minister and his party stepped off the train at Woodend, a frozen white landscape greeted them. Snow had been falling on Mount Macedon. Snow on the mount was not unusual, but it was uncommon for the areas surrounding Macedon to be so heavily covered with snow. It had been a bitterly cold winter. John had the honour of greeting the official party at the station. He shook hands with all the men and showed them to his buggy. When they arrived at Newham, they trudged through the snow to the entrance of the hall where they met with the Shire President and the remaining Councillors from the Newham Shire Council.

The Minister was here to meet with the locals to hear their opposing views about use of the Hanging Rock reserve. Horse racing at the rock was under threat yet again because of the need to extend the track to meet the ever-increasing requirements of the Victorian Racing Commission. Even the new track on the East side of the rock had never been particularly safe, and many amateur jockeys had come to grief on race day. Recently, a jockey had been thrown from his horse and collided with one of the huge gums surrounding the track. He had died as a result of his injuries. John felt that this really should be the end of it. The death of a jockey surely should sound the death knell for horse racing at Hanging Rock.

But the racing club had petitioned the government to permit the extension of the track. Without it, the Victorian Racing Commission would not allow racing to continue at Hanging Rock. And of course, there was access to the water that the farmers still considered to be their right. The ramblers and pleasure seekers just wanted to enjoy the rock for their leisure. The same old arguments raged on.

The Minister was well aware of these wide-reaching opinions and issues but John was very pleased that despite the fiery reception that the Minister knew he would probably receive, he had accepted the council's invitation to come and talk to the locals to see if the issue could be resolved. But John was concerned. He knew a storm was brewing in the small country hall.

The Minister and his party entered the hall with the councillors. The Shire President rose to address the several hundred people who had gathered for the event.

"Thank you all for attending," he began. "We are privileged today to welcome The Minister for Lands, Mr Albert Tucker."

Before the words were out of his mouth, there were derisive jeers from the assembled locals.

"Please, hold your comments until the appropriate time." The noise level fell again. "I would now like to introduce the Minister and ask him to address the assembly."

The Minister rose to address the raucous crowd.

"Can I please have your attention?" he said. "I would like to try to help you all to come to an agreement on the best use of this wonderful asset that you have in your community."

Again, the crowd jeered.

The Minister tried again.

"Surely the community can agree that there is a place for all in the Hanging Rock Reserve."

"There is no place for excessive consumption of alcohol in our community," came a loud retort from the crowd. The crowd again erupted, some sections cheering loudly, whilst many others jeered and booed.

The Minister tried several more times with the Shire President periodically trying to control the crowd.

The Minister gave up. "I thought the people of this community were a civilised bunch, but I see that is not the case. I shall make no further attempts to talk sense into you."

He left the stage, followed by the Councillors.

"Please Minister," said the Shire President, "we really need to resolve this issue."

"Well Sir, I don't think there can be a resolution whilst tempers are raised as they are today. The only suggestion I have is to maintain the status quo. There will be no permit from the Government for the improvement to the racecourse." And with that, he and his party left the small community to its own devices and trudged back through the snow to catch the train back to Melbourne.

After the meeting, John Marlowe and Harold Langdon sat by the open fire in the comfortable sitting room of John's spacious timber home. Elizabeth entered the room carrying the tea tray. The men smiled at her as she poured tea from the teapot, kept warm by its knitted tea cosy. They had smelt the delicious aroma coming from the kitchen and were delighted to see that the tea tray contained oatmeal cookies straight from the oven. Elizabeth took a seat by the fire.

"Well, tell me. How did it go?" she asked.

"It is depressing, Elizabeth, my dear," answered John. "We did not make any progress. In fact, the Minister left in a huff, would you believe? It seems there can be no resolution. The community just cannot seem to reach consensus on this issue." Both men stared gloomily into the fire.

"Poor Father would be devastated to know that even eleven years after his death, there has still been no resolution."

And there was no resolution. The dispute would continue for years.

Epilogue

1910 Hesket

Rachael entered the cemetery feeling a sadness that she could not fully explain. She had been only 10 years old when her grandfather had died and she barely remembered her grandmother. She wandered down the gravel pathway between the neat rows of headstones. Tall gums and thick bush surrounded the cemetery and seemed to provide natural protection for the graves. The wind rustled in the leaves. It felt like they were whispering to her in the quiet of the cemetery.

She wasn't sure where the graves of her grandparents were, despite her father explaining their location. It took her some time to find them. Eventually, she was looking at the place where her grandparents lay at rest. She read the inscription on the headstone.

Robert Blayney

1825 - 1902

and his beloved wife

Charlotte

1826 - 1898

Rachael wondered what they would both make of her decision. She had met and fallen in love with Ernest Bennett, the great grandson of Samuel Marlowe. Her mother had related all the stories about the conflict that had divided the community, as well as many stories of their own family conflicts. She worried about what Ernest's family must think of the match. Ernest had reassured her that he didn't care what they thought. He wanted to let bygones be bygones. He was well aware of the opposing sides their families had taken in the long running dispute over the Hanging Rock reserve. He was also well aware of all her family's many transgressions and court appearances. He didn't care what her family's background was. All he knew was that he loved her and wanted to marry her.

She left the cemetery and mounted her pony. Her Uncle Edward had bred the spirited horse and she felt privileged to own such an animal. She turned the horse for home. She must talk to her mother.

When she arrived home, her mother was toiling over the washtub.

"Mother, would you like a cup of tea?" she asked. "You look exhausted. Please take a break now. I would like to talk to you anyway."

"Very well dear." Rachael's mother wiped her brow with the back of her hand and dried her hands on the towel hanging from the hook near the washtub.

She sat down at the table and let her daughter make the tea. When both women had a steaming cup of tea in front of them, Rachael raised the subject of her match with Ernest.

"Mother, I am concerned that Ernie's family will think that I am not good enough for him."

"Indeed! And why would they think that?" replied her mother with raised eyebrows.

"Oh Mother, you know what I mean. Our family is hardly a match for the very religious Marlowe family."

"Well, I would not agree with that. Your father's family came here with nothing and built up everything we now enjoy. I think your grandfather would be quite disappointed to think that you don't think we are good enough for the likes of the Marlowes. He spent much of his life proving that he was worthy to live freely in this country."

"I am sorry, Mother. I know you are right, but it doesn't change the fact that they probably don't think I am good enough for Ernie."

"My girl, you must stop this. You are every bit as good as any other young lass. What does Ernest say about your concerns?"

"He says that his family will welcome me. And that he doesn't care what anyone thinks anyway. He says that it is all ancient history and we need to move on. "

"Well, there you are then. You have nothing to worry about. That young man loves you and that is all that matters."

The wedding took place on a cold, blustery day in July 1910. The two families were united.

The End

Author's Note

This book is a work of fiction based on real life events. It is inspired by the true story of my ancestors who settled at Hanging Rock. When writing a work such as this the balance between sticking as closely as possible to the facts (as they are known at the time) and writing an entertaining story is a delicate balance.

I wanted to record this story as factually as I could but there are so many gaps in my knowledge of these people and so many assumptions that needed to be made.

For example, I have not yet been able to discover whether the family went to the goldfields and made a small fortune. But I decided to make the assumption that as they lived so close to Mount Alexander, at least one member of the family would surely have tried their luck. Another thing that points to this is that their large family seems to have prospered reasonably quickly and were able to set up farms and businesses in Hesket and Melbourne.

I took the decision to change the names of all the characters, with the exception of one or two historical figures who are peripheral to the story. In doing so I have taken much license with the story, however much of it remains based in fact.

The conflict that surrounds the Hanging Rock Water and Recreation Reserve occured over many decades. I hope the reader is not too disappointed that this conflict did not have final resolution by the end of the book as it was ongoing for years. However it can be noted that horseraces are still run at the Hanging Rock racecourse to this day.

As I say I have not yet been able to find certain facts to complete the whole story. But as family historians will know, the story is never really complete. As more resources become available online and as I have more time to research, new facts will continue to emerge.

For now, this is the story so far. I hope that you have enjoyed it.

Acknowledgments

I would like to start by acknowledging the Traditional Owners of the land on which this story is set. Hanging Rock is located near the traditional boundary between three Aboriginal Traditional Owner groups – the Woi Wurrung (Wurundjeri), the Djaara and the Taungurung. I pay my respects to their elders, past present and emerging.

In my research for this book, I was unable to find direct evidence of any contact my ancestors had with the Traditional Owners, however I acknowledge that simply by being there, they contributed to the dispossession of this land.

I have been gathering sources for this story since I first commenced researching my family history some 15 years ago. But there were several works that contributed significantly to my research.

The first was William Blandowski's Illustrated Encyclopedia of Aboriginal Australia. The wonderful illustrations and commentary in this book really assisted with understanding how the Aboriginal People lived and cared for the land for so long before European settlement. This work was recommended to me by Delta Lucille Freedman from the Wurundjeri Woi Wurrung Corporation. However my story has ended up not including significant reference to the Traditional Owners as I did not feel well enough informed to tell their story.

I also relied on several local histories written by members of the Woodend and District Heritage Society which provided invaluable sources.

But by far the best source was Hanging Rock – A History by Chris McConville.

I am grateful to all of these historians who have provided so much background information for my story.

Trove newspapers were also a wonderful source and I used these resources extensively.

I would like to thank my editor, Cecile Shanahan, whose patience was certainly appreciated as she guided me through my first edit. She helped me to find ways to write an entertaining and well structured story, despite my determination to keep the story as factual as possible.

Thank you to my early readers, Hannah Thomson and Heather Kelly. Your contributions and comments helped to make my story better.

My cover was designed by Douglas Thomson at High Voltage Studio. Thank you.

About the Author

Pauline Wilson lives in Yarrawonga in North East Victoria on the banks of the Murray River. She is a writer and family historian who loves learning and research. She writes historical fiction based on true stories of her ancestors. When she is not writing she likes to read, research her ancestors and take long walks. *Conflict at Hanging Rock* is her first novel.

Connect on Instagram (@paulinemareewilson) or Facebook (@paulinewilsonauthor) or sign up for the latest news at www.paulinewilson.com.au/news

REVIEWS

Did you enjoy this book? You can make a big difference.

Honest reviews are the most powerful tools for getting my book noticed. So if you enjoyed this book I would I be very grateful if you could spend just a couple of minutes leaving a short review where ever you purchased this book.

Breaking Free

by Pauline Wilson

Nineteen-year-old Annie finds herself incarcerated in Kew Mental Asylum in 1894, her memories shrouded in a fog of confusion. As the months unfold Annie navigates the grim reality of her surroundings and forms a friendship with fellow inmate Helena who helps her come to terms with her past and consider a future beyond the asylum.

Annie's journey begins with the loss of her mother at the tender age of five, her father's grief leaving little room for her in his heart. With the arrival of a new stepmother, Annie becomes responsible for her younger half-siblings. Seeking solace in her catholic faith, she comes under the influence of a strict and unforgiving priest, further shaping her turmultuous path.

The matron of the asylum becomes a beacon of hope for Annie, employing all her strength and influence to help Annie break free from her nightmarish reality. In a world where women's voices are beginning to rise, the matron's deter-mination to champion Annie's cause, underscores the shifts occuring in society. Amidst the darkness, Annie's journey to rediscover herself, intertwines with the matron's fight for justice, offering a poignant portrayal of friendship, resilience and the unstoppable march towards progress.

But will the man she loves be there to support her as she fights to escape the horrors of the institution? This emotional and powerful story exposes the abuses and mistreatment that were all too common in mental institutions in the late 1800s.

Available now in all online bookstores or buy direct at: www.paulinewilson.com.au

www.ingramcontent.com/pod-product-compliance
Lightning Source LLC
Chambersburg PA
CBHW020008140726
47904CB00018B/2128